PETER PEARS

A Tribute on His 75th Birthday

Peter Pears with Benjamin Britten in 1967, in the Library at the Red House

PETER PEARS

A Tribute on His 75th Birthday

EDITED BY

MARION THORPE

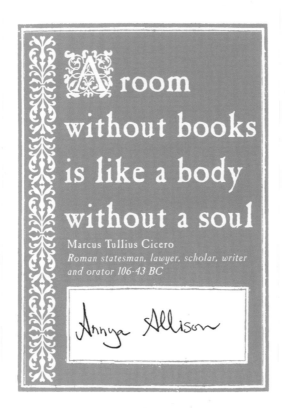

A room without books is like a body without a soul

Marcus Tullius Cicero
Roman statesman, lawyer, scholar, writer and orator 106-43 BC

Annya Allison

A BRITTEN–PEARS LIBRARY PUBLICATION

FABER MUSIC LIMITED IN ASSOCIATION WITH
THE BRITTEN ESTATE

First published in 1985
by Faber Music Limited
3 Queen Square London WC1N 3AU
in association with The Britten Estate
The Red House Aldeburgh Suffolk IP15 5PZ

Design: James Butler MSIAD
Typeset in Palatino 10/13 by Goodfellow & Egan, Cambridge
Printed in Great Britain by
BAS Printers Limited, Stockbridge, Hampshire

British Library Cataloguing in Publication Data
A Tribute to Sir Peter Pears on his 75th birthday.
1. Pears, Peter   2. Singers—Great Britain—
Biography   3. Opera—Great Britain—Biography
I. Thorpe, Marion   II. Pears, Peter
782.1'092'4   ML420.P3/
ISBN 0-571-10063-5

Contents

List of Contributors

List of Illustrations

The engravings on pages 9, 87, 93 and 97 are by Reynolds Stone and are reproduced by kind permission of Janet Stone.

Jacket illustration: Peter Pears, pencil drawing by Don Bachardy, 1976

Preface and Acknowledgements

The idea of a 'Festschrift' for Peter Pears's 75th birthday on June 22nd 1985 was conceived by the Trustees of the Britten–Pears Foundation and the contents were compiled during the autumn of 1984. We would like to thank all those who have contributed in various ways towards making the book as comprehensive of Peter Pears's life as possible. Some omissions were inevitable for reasons of absence, time and space, but we have tried to represent those missing amongst Peter's closest colleagues by photographs or mentions in other ways. The signatories of the Council and Staff of the Aldeburgh Foundation, the Staff of the Britten–Pears Library and the Directors of Faber Music were correct at the time of going to print.

Amongst those whose help and co-operation we acknowledge and to whom we offer our thanks are:

Rosamund Strode, Archivist, as well as Paul Wilson and his staff at the Britten–Pears Library for research and collation of material. Their work was not made easier by the fact that this book was to be a complete surprise, so that certain facts were difficult to verify without recourse to the one person who would know, namely Peter himself.

All composers and artists or their heirs for allowing their works to be reproduced; and the owners of some of these works: HRH Princess of Hesse and the Rhine, Mel and Rhiannòn Gooding, Lilian Sheepshanks and indeed Peter Pears, unknown to himself.

Martin Cooper and Patrick Carnegy for their translations, and Sergei Hackel for typing the Russian text.

Jill Burrows for preparing the material for publication; James Butler, the designer, and Piers Hembry of Faber Music who assisted its production.

All photographers, including the following, whose pictures are reproduced in the three collages: E. Nash (New York, 1940); Houston Rogers (*Toilus and Cressida*, 1954; *The Bartered Bride*, 1955; *The Mastersingers of Nuremberg*, 1957); Kurt Hutton (*Les Mamelles de Tirésias*, 1958); Zoe Dominic (*The Burning Fiery Furnace*, 1966; *Idomeneo*, 1967); Angus McBean (*Peter Grimes*, 1949; *The Rape of Lucretia*, 1946; *Albert Herring*, 1947); Maria Austria (*The Beggar's Opera*, 1948); Roger Wood (*Billy Budd*, 1951); Herbert Nott (*The Turn of the Screw*, 1957); Nigel Luckhurst (*Death in Venice*, 1973); others, whose names we were unable to trace; and the copyright owners or holders of some of these pictures: Peter Hutton, The Harvard Theatre Collection, Particam, the BBC, The Victoria and Albert Museum. In the case of any inadvertent omissions, we offer our apologies and shall be glad to hear from the copyright owners involved.

And finally Peter Pears himself, whose life and art has brought about such a generous response from his colleagues and friends.

London, March 1985   MARION THORPE

PETER:
CELEBRATED BY
HIS FRIENDS

HM Queen Elizabeth The Queen Mother, Patron of the Aldeburgh Festival, with Peter
Pears at a Musical Reception held at St. James's Palace on 20 March 1984

CLARENCE HOUSE
S.W. 1

    As Patron of the Aldeburgh Festival and
as a friend of long-standing, I am delighted to pay
my tribute to Sir Peter Pears on his 75th birthday.

    Through his worldwide range of musical
achievements, he has become a legend in his own
lifetime, and all those involved in the affairs of
the Aldeburgh Foundation must, I am sure, feel
deeply grateful to Sir Peter for his unfailing
inspiration through the years.

    I offer him my heartfelt congratulations and
warmest good wishes for the future.

Elizabeth R

Janet Baker

In London the other day I saw a man riding in a taxi. There was something about the set of the head, the clear-cut features that caught my attention. 'It's Peter,' I thought, but the next moment realized it wasn't and the taxi with its unknown occupant was swallowed up in the traffic.

What is it, I wonder, about old friends that tears at the heart strings? Memories, I suppose, all those incidents shared over so many years. Such people become even more precious as time passes because they mirror our lives as well as their own and we do the same for them.

For performers there is something special about one's colleagues, something in the shared agony and joy of public life that forges a unique bond.

There were occasions in the early days of my career when I have walked into some freezing church and seen that beloved figure sitting on a pew in his tweed overcoat waiting for his turn to rehearse. One always felt uplifted by the thought of a performance ahead graced by the artistry of Peter Pears. He must have had this presence from the first. He still has it, that certain style, refinement, graciousness; that great intelligence and musicality which made his appearance in a line-up of soloists a guarantee of the highest standards because where Peter went, he encouraged us to follow; his knowledge and experience freely offered and his advice given with such tender concern. Only a great artist has the unselfishness to help another singer; only the kindest of human beings the tact to do it without at the same time destroying confidence.

Once, we were doing Bach cantatas together in Leeds Parish Church. After hearing me rehearse some recitative Peter talked to me at length about the necessity for the rhythmic accuracy required even when certain words must be accentuated because of the sense. I saw immediately what he meant; I had been pulling the structure of the bars about in my anxiety to make the speech as meaningful as possible. He showed me how the words could be even more effective when placed properly on the beat as Bach had written it and ever since I have felt indescribable joy when singing 'speech' as he encouraged me to do; firmly held within the safe hands of Bach, one is free, because of the security, to soar above it, freedom and discipline working hand in hand.

In 1967 the English Opera Group was touring Russia; at short notice Ben and Peter asked me to do a performance of *Abraham and Isaac* with them at a concert, I forget just where, probably Leningrad. It was an exciting but daunting prospect since the piece was new to me and a first performance with the composer and original Abraham was diving in at the deep end! I need not have worried; with Ben at the piano and Peter at my side they held me firm, rather like the filling in a sandwich! It was an unforgettable experience, which, once again, brought home to me how much every kind of music depends on rhythm because they themselves were such marvellous examples of this ideal.

Peter has always had a remarkable sensitivity for words, his ability to colour them with the voice equally remarkable. Both these qualities are so developed in him that I suspect his love of painting has something to do with this aspect of his singing. His visual sense must have sharpened his feeling for word-painting or perhaps it is the other way round. Anyway, he is a wonderful teacher because of his respect both for words and the integrity of his approach to a score.

To grow old is to take part in a great mystery. Time reveals us to one another more and more clearly; there is a deepening nobility as personality gives way and the essence of a person comes to the surface. Watching Peter talking in the house of some friends a little while ago it was obvious to me that this process is now flowering in him. He has lived many years, of suffering and of joy; he has conquered illness, served his profession; he remains the superb artist in his teaching; life has written on his still beautiful face an unmistakable message for all to read, 'Here is a great human being.'

Steuart Bedford

THE STRUGGLE WITH THE WORD

'Should I give up the fruitless struggle with the word?' Thus exclaims Aschenbach near the start of the opera *Death in Venice*. I do not think that I am betraying any professional secrets when I say that Peter would have been only too happy to answer this question in the affirmative, not from any drying up of inspiration, which was Aschenbach's trouble, but simply because of his own particular difficulty in remembering that 'word'.

With Peter this problem would usually manifest itself with his forgetting not the whole sentence but just one or two constituent words, the noun, adjective or verb: that he was almost always ready with a more than satisfactory alternative is just one, albeit a small one, of the fascinating sidelines of his art to which I would like to pay tribute.

Peter very rarely dried up totally on stage though he did have a blank spot about Nebuchadnezzar's opening line in *The Burning Fiery Furnace*, 'Adept in

Benjamin Britten: *Death in Venice*, Op. 88.
A page from the composition sketch, with Aschenbach's recitative.
Autograph manuscript

magic', which was probably due to the unlikely nature of the line and its apparent illogicality. Also sheer nonsense was very rare, 'Back Collatinus!' in *The Rape of Lucretia* being the exception that proves the rule. When a line did escape him altogether, and he was reduced to singing what he himself referred to as 'verbal chewing-gum', he somehow managed, by stage presence and force of personality, to convince the audience that their puzzled incomprehension was due entirely to a lack of concentration on their part.

Occasionally he would start a word and then suddenly realize that he should be singing another, changing in mid-stream with interesting results. For example, he once started the word 'fate' and realized before reaching the letter 't' that he should have been singing the word 'case'. So what the audience heard was 'desperate indeed is his face'.

However, it is the spontaneous invention of new words to suit the emergency that turns this weakness into an amazing source of strength, making his struggle with the word far from fruitless. Often the alternative became the preferred version and was taken over by the librettist. *Death in Venice* positively teems with examples, but the process was already well established by the time of the first of the church operas, *Curlew River*. 'It ill becomes you Curlew Ferryman such incivility' sings the Madwoman. But Peter would invariably produce 'It ill befits . . .' showing an unconscious preference for a double 'f' alliteration rather than the hard double 'c': then, not always being certain of what it was that ill befitted the Ferryman, he would sometimes substitute 'importunity'. One only needs to call upon poetic licence to defend this.

In over thirty-five performances (and the attendant rehearsals) that I must have conducted with Peter of *Death in Venice*, the wealth of spontaneous creativity that he exhibited could almost have a volume to itself. To illustrate the process I would ask the reader to imagine himself faced with the sentence '. . . but the truth is that it has been precipitated by a sudden desire for the unknown' and further to imagine that he has forgotten the word 'precipitated'. How many of us could without hesitation read the line substituting an alternative four-syllable word? In two successive American performances Peter first gave 'accelerated' and then at the next performance to my amazement found a second alternative, 'initiated', both without the slightest hesitation.

Time and again an adjective would desert him and an immediate appropriate replacement be found – 'that absurd obstinate gondolier' became an 'absurd truculent gondolier' or 'so I had to mock myself as the crestfallen lover' became 'starcrossed lover'.

But the masterpiece has always seemed to me his version of the line 'the city fathers are rarely so serious'. Coming to the line at a comparatively late rehearsal for the première, Peter suddenly substituted 'seldom' for 'rarely', which with 'serious' makes a nice alliteration. However, having begun with 'seldom', he proceeded to trump his own ace with 'solicitous'. In the printed libretto the line now reads, 'the city fathers are seldom so solicitous'.

George Behrend

SOME MEMORABLE MOMENTS

Perhaps Peter Burra knew he had started something, when he introduced you to Ben. But it never dawned on me, when through him I separately met both of you, that Ben's friendship would last so long, nor that you would give me countless ecstatic moments in concert hall or opera house. Now I can thank you publicly.

There was never a dull moment, from your 1936 Marlborough Town Hall concert with Bruce Hylton-Stewart, which I attended clandestinely, despite H.-S. being the College music master. Nor an angry moment: you looked after Ben so graciously, putting up with his austere ways, like those frightful school forms at his dining table. Most people never fully understood that Ben really cared most for his genius; his work came before everything.

Surprise moments: at Glyndebourne in 1947, the world première of *Herring* was even conducted in my socks! Clothes were rationed then, like petrol. No traffic made driving you about on tour a marvellous pleasure.

Hilarious moments, too, but also moments of *Angst* – German words are *de rigeur* here. When still recovering from shingles, you had to help Ben push the car in the middle of Newcastle, on that 1950 concert tour based at Drymen's Buchanan Arms. Before we left Melbury Road, Erwin Stein read of our Scottish tour in the *Evening Standard*. I remarked it did not mention me. 'It will,' said Ben instantly, 'when we have the accident!'

This *Festschrift* may come as a surprise; it certainly surprised me to be asked to write something. I did not even realize it was your 75th birthday, but it's over thirty years since last I handed your passport to a frontier policeman. Customs were far more fussy then. A Harwich man demanded to see me – the car was full of locked suitcases without keys! Everyone else arrived later, by train. But all he wanted was Ben's photograph.

Ben gave me much good advice about writing. Unfortunately, he chose to do so in a Dinant canoe. Instead of listening properly, I was concerned with capsizing into the Meuse – and what you'd say then!

These days, I'm the *éminence grise* on the Orient Express (!). Nobody cared about it in 1966, when you generously let me quote *Armenian Diary* in my book *Yatakli-Vagon* (Turkish for *wagons-lits*) that has just been used for the Nostalgic Istanbul Orient Express press handouts. My Zürich friends of Intraflug have run the train for the last nine years, so it's nice Ben has immortalized *wagons-lits* in

Death in Venice. Myfanwy told me it was meant to be Cook's: but learned libretto study (not a musicologist's monopoly) conclusively proves otherwise!

All over Britain, people are celebrating 22 June with music far superior to these prosaic good wishes. Assuredly Ben would have approved of 22 June as European Music Day of European Music Year.

Lennox Berkeley

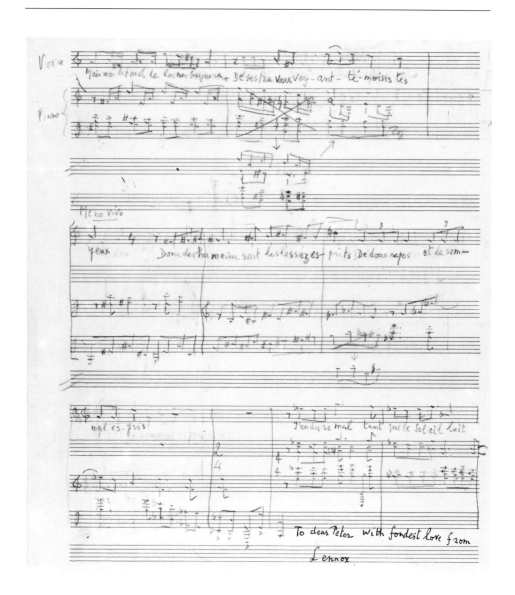

Sonnet (1982), Words by Louise Labé. Written for Hugues Cuénod at the suggestion of Peter Pears for the Aldeburgh Festival celebration of Cuénod's 80th birthday, *For Hugues Cuénod, with love*, Jubilee Hall, 26 June 1982
Autograph manuscript

Peter Bowring and the Members of the Council of the Aldeburgh Foundation

The Members of the Council of the Aldeburgh Foundation send you their warmest greetings and best wishes on your 75th birthday. Your tireless efforts and your unique artistic contribution have given the Festival and all that the Foundation stands for the highest national and international prestige. We, in company with your many friends everywhere, will always be deeply grateful to you.

PETER BOWRING	ISADOR CAPLAN	PATRICIA MADDOCKS
EUGENE MELVILLE	RICHARD CAVE	COLIN MATTHEWS
PETER DU SAUTOY	DAVID HECKELS	DONALD MITCHELL
JOHN JACOB	JOHN HUTCHISON	PRUDENCE PENN
DAVID BATTERBEE	WILLIAM JACOB	MARION THORPE

The Staff of the Aldeburgh Foundation

Every member of the Aldeburgh Foundation's staff offers you warmest greetings and congratulations on your 75th birthday. We are deeply grateful for your continuing direction and inspiration and for all the hard work you unstintingly devote to the Britten–Pears School and to the planning of the Festival programme. We all celebrate with you.

KENNETH BAIRD	PERDITA HUNT	RUTH PEVERILL
MOIRA BENNETT	MARK KEMBALL	HARRY PIPE
KEITH CABLE	BOB LING	JOYCE SMITH
VIRGINIA CALDWELL	DORIS LING	LLOYDA SWATLAND
DON CANHAM	CHRIS NICHOLSON	PENNY SYDENHAM
ILSE EDWARDS	LYLA OSBISTON	SALLY TONG
SUSAN HARRISON	JOHN OWEN	DEBORAH WALDEN

William Burrell

Dear Peter,

Happy Birthday – or should I say 'Sir Peter'? – where have all the years gone to? One of the first things I always remember was meeting George Harewood at the breakfast table one morning at yours and when I went in the first thing he said was, 'My name is George. How are you, Bill?' And we shook hands. This was my first encounter with Royalty and then the Hesses came along and what a wonderful crowd of friends you and Ben had and have. I am sure all past and present are wishing you all the very best: just to name a few, there was dear Imogen Holst, the Steins, Otakar Kraus, Joan Cross, Morgan Forster, William Plomer, Basil Douglas, Basil Coleman, Leslie Periton, John Cranko, Trevor Anthony, John Piper, Mary Potter, Kathleen Ferrier and so many more as we all know. I am sure that they are all with me past and present to recall such a day as you are going to celebrate on your 75th.

Do you recall when Ben said he had got a surprise for me and asked what I thought it might be and I said he was going to marry Mary Potter, and did he laugh and did you! In actual fact it was the time when you changed houses from the Crag Path to Red House. Also the night during the Festival when you, Ben and I do not know how many Lords, Earls, Dukes, you name it, went out in my Boat to a large corvette that was lying off Aldeburgh and all that drink we had between us! We returned in the early hours of the morning. It was a flat calm, a full moon, one of the days that you hardly ever see in this part of the world, and would the engine start? It was either me too drunk or I do not know what; but anyhow we could not start the engine. Do you remember at that time when you sang better than at any Opera and everybody cheered and laughed and we had a whale of a time?

I often think of those days and also of our trip up the Rhine and your guests were Basil Coleman, Arthur Oldham, myself, John, Nipper – poor Nipper sadly gone, amongst so many of our dear friends. Also the night when I came in through the front door and on this particular night I think nearly all the nobility of Aldeburgh were in the Drawing Room and Ben said, 'Hello, Bill, I think you know everybody here' and as you know in those days it was not easy for us to mix with that class of people or that class of people to mix with us. When Ben was made a Lord and I asked him whether I should come in backwards, frontwards or bow or what and he said 'Don't be a damn fool', and he asked Rita to go and get all his regalia that the Queen had given him and what a

Wilfred Owen 'All a poet can do is
warn'   B.B. worked after he
left U.S.A   to articulate his ᴀʟʟ feelings

'Passage to India' (read)

Paul Bunyan got off to a false start
B.B said Vergil Thompson was an
'old stinker'
Christopher I sherwood was convince
that the story of 'Peter Grimes' was
a no-hoper as an opera. (that was
before the hero was toned down from that
of Crabbs poem.)
Grimes is a meloncoly man
hence the meloncoly of the music
The Borough Theme is in B♭.
Read John Gill - "Queer Noises"?

In an artical in U.S.A B.B mentioned
Walton getting away from Parry (Pastrol/
and many others   music

wonderful thing it was. I shall never forget those happy days.

Well, Peter, I hope you will have lots and lots more Birthdays to come and that we can travel down memory lane together as I have done in this short note to you. When I was invited to write a few words for this Birthday Book for you I was so pleased to be asked but alas me not being a letter-writer!!! But I think I know about you and Ben over the forty years that I have known you and it has made me very proud and very pleased once again to just be asked to write a few words of our past and friendship.

All my love,

BILL

Jill Burrows

Miss Hudson and Gilda arriving in the courtyard office, slightly out of breath, having quickened their collective step if not lengthened their collective stride, pursued – as they thought – across the golf course by some sinister figure. On learning it was you: 'Me and Gilda don't talk to strange men.'

The pause in Jersild's 'Puzzle from Wonderland', still, head to one side, waiting, demonstrating that thinking and listening can be the same thing.

The inexhaustible supply of pink felt-tip pens.

Playing a continuous and anarchic game of grown-ups' patience with the Red House paintings, defeating the foolhardy efficiency of the insurers' room-by-room lists.

Earl Grey 'stiffened' with a little Darjeeling.

Landing on the right *title* for Festival events, as well as the right works and the right artists.

Reading the poems of Sylvia Townsend Warner, finding the warmth *and* the strangeness in them:

> Who chooses the music, turns the page,
> Waters the geraniums on the window-ledge?
>
> . . . I am his to command,
> My times are in his hand.
> Once in a dream I called him Azrael.

13

A transcribed interview with you in which *Die schöne Müllerin* appeared as 'show in a million' – in your case, an accurate description. (The same transcript unearthed a hitherto unknown major character in *A Midsummer Night's Dream* – Overarm.)

The scarf draped round the neck that signals a sore throat but does nothing to protect it.

Commissioning music for other people to enjoy.

The pocket dictating machine that saw its vocation as recording the inside of your briefcase.

Knowing that a cat called 'Cenci' may be properly and intimately addressed as 'Beatrice'.

The last-minute rush.

Supporting the Peace Pledge Union through thick and thin.

Performances in opera, oratorio and song that taught audience after audience 'compassion with the abyss'.

Converting me at a time when I was convinced that opera was *really stupid*. In a single moment – on a television screen, a Madwoman pleading with a Ferryman – teaching me that a certain combination of image and idea, experience and emotion can be expressed *in no other way*.

For all this, and so much more, thank you, Peter.

Alan Bush

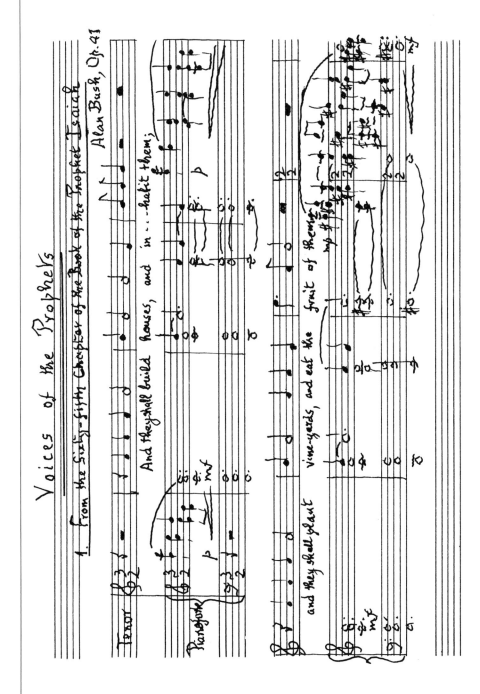

Voices of the Prophets, Op. 41, 'From the Sixty-fifth Chapter of the Book of the Prophet Isaiah'
Autograph manuscript

Richard Butt

My dear Peter,

Translated into terms of silver, gold and diamonds, not to mention rubies, I don't really know what is the appropriate gift for a 75th birthday, though it does offer a special moment to renew our expressions of affection and gratitude to you for having enriched us for so long with so much that is good and joyous.

For me it started about forty years ago with the *Serenade*, the British Folk Songs and *Les Illuminations*. Then, a recital with Kathleen Ferrier and Ben at the Central Hall, Westminster that included 'Waft her, angels', and it was in the singing, and the playing, of that single Handel aria followed shortly by a *Matthew Passion* with van Beinum that one became aware of a new doorway into music. If such a thing can be explained – it can't of course any more than it's possible to explain a daffodil or an apricot – it would be to do with the heart and the imagination – creating the magic that steals over us, adding new dimensions to thought and feeling; perhaps you should have played Prospero. Bach, Handel and Schütz, all with their special birthdays this year too, and Schumann, Schubert and Purcell have become 'Aldeburgh composers', part of the feast that keeps us from our gardens each June, a feast that feeds us with sound and sight as well as strawberries, sole straight from the sea and asparagus.

Your generosity to the Birmingham Bach Society has been wonderfully supportive and encouraging, but I know we are by no means the only ones who benefit from your kindness. Once when we talked about the Bach Passions you said how important it was to find the tunes and the shapes in the recitatives, and the terrible problem of trying to make it work in English. Do you think it is possible to get any closer to Bach's musical text with an acceptable English version or are we too conditioned by the sound of the Authorized Version?

But it's not just the recits in the Passions. Recently while preparing a parallel English text for the audience at one of our Bach concerts I came across the following in one of the cantatas –

> Alles, alles was wir sehen,
> das muss fallen und vergehen.

> Days of labour, days of sorrow,
> Here today and gone tomorrow.

– and there must be a lot more like that waiting to be sung.

Then to the words and the music we must add the great gallery of unforgettable characters, from Grimes to Aschenbach, and that memorable Idomeneo (shades of Jephtha!) and the unlikely role of the apprentice David in *Die Meistersinger*. Now there are other apprentices, in your own school, who, by kind insistence, will be helped and encouraged through the doors opened for them. Whatever they may find there, whatever they achieve, they will, like those who started the journey earlier, be thinking of you on your special day with love and thankfulness.

Long may you appear and inspire, and startle us with your own immortal fire. Happy Birthday!

As always,

RICHARD

Joan and Isador Caplan

Dear Peter,

Impossible to believe that this is a greeting for your 75th birthday. I suppose the best thing about growing old with friends is that they remain, as does oneself of course, eternally the same.

It is also a thank-you letter – a thank you for all the enormous pleasure your singing, acting and reading have given Isador and me these past forty years. For us you have been unique among singers, not least because you imparted to your audience your own delight whether you were singing from the vast repertory that Ben composed for you, or the works of other great composers: even the most difficult pieces (for the relatively uninformed ear) became immediately available to us.

We have been very fortunate in our musical mentors – first dear Erwin Stein (who said you were the most musicianly of all our singers) and then you and Ben. We are ever conscious of our debt to our musical trinity, and it is marvellous to have the opportunity to say thank you in print.

Yours affectionately,

JOAN

May I add a postscript to Joan's letter to you, for three reasons?

The first is to express our deepest admiration for your and Ben's unswerving commitment to peace and non-violence, which has been such an inspiration to us, as to so many others – as witness the 'Mass offered for the peace of mankind on the 71st Anniversary of the birthday of Benjamin Britten' at Westminster Cathedral.

The second is the Britten–Pears School for Advanced Musical Studies, where to this day you continue to transmit the musical skills and standards that you and Ben evolved over the years, both in your own work and in working with the younger singers and musicians of promise whom you engaged for the Aldeburgh Festival from its earliest beginnings.

The third is your part in founding the Britten–Pears Library, and in nurturing its development into an important research institution, not only for Ben's music, but also for your Library of English Song, built up by you throughout your career, and including many rare and important books and scores. The Library also bears witness to your sensitive judgement as a collector of contemporary painting and other art objects, many acquired from artists who were still awaiting the recognition they eventually achieved.

It has been both a joy and a privilege to work with and for you in these and other fields all these years.

Much love,

ISADOR

Basil Coleman

My dear Peter,

Thinking of you and your 75th birthday has taken me back to the first time we met, in the house you shared with Sophie and Erwin Stein in Paddington in 1948! It was a most memorable evening, with you singing Macheath and Ben simulating all the orchestral parts on the piano during the first play-through of his realization of *The Beggar's Opera*.

Apart from all the other wonderful working periods I have spent with you, particularly on *Billy Budd*, both in the opera house and on television, *Gloriana* and *The Turn of the Screw*, so many more shared experiences come flooding back. Our journey up the Rhine in a converted naval motor launch in 1951 is one, an idea of yours and Ben's as a break before the start of *Billy Budd* rehearsals soon afterwards.

Do you remember leaving Aldeburgh at dawn, the Alde so smooth that you decided to prepare a sumptuous first breakfast, the full English variety, for all seven of us? I acted as assistant, and we did rather well considering the size of the stove. However, by the time we had passed Shingle Street and entered the open sea, my appetite and yours were distinctly less keen. We spent the day in the fresh air as we crossed over to Holland.

Incidentally, I think that holiday provided you with one of your rare opportunities to indulge your culinary enthusiasm. You enjoyed shopping *en route*, then creating delectable dishes on board. You were always ready to try new things; Ben, I suspect, would have preferred Miss Hudson's less exotic creations sometimes.

Most bridges were still down and rebuilding of towns on the Rhine in Holland and Germany had hardly begun. Do you remember the German who helped us refuel in Düsseldorf, cautiously telling us he had been a prisoner of war in England? It was a moving moment. I recall Ben, after one of our onshore walks, remarking on the beauty of the German people and how much closer he felt to them in temperament than to our, geographically, much nearer neighbours.

There were anxious moments, apart from those provided by the occasional river rapids. Those long lines of heavily laden barges, eight of them often, hauled by tugs, which made for the deeper channels, irrespective of traffic rules, could be rather frightening. In Cologne we were hemmed in by two sets of them, a severe test of our crew, John Burrell and his Aldeburgh fisherman brother Billy!

We arrived in Koblenz on a very hot day and climbed to the top of the Ehrenbreitstein. You chose the perfect wine, a beautifully chilled Mosel, which we drank overlooking the superb view of where the river, from which the wine took its name, joins the Rhine.

We reached Bingen before having to turn back, no mean feat in that small boat. It was a memorable time, made even more so for me for sharing your and Ben's marvellously fresh response to everything. Luckily you will never lose that. Like your sense of humour, it is very special. They are just two of your great gifts which have made it such a pleasure to be in your company always.

Dear Peter, may you have a very happy birthday.

BASIL

Aaron Copland

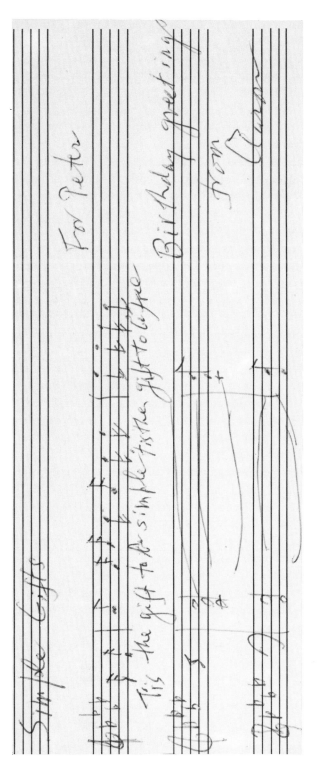

'Simple Gifts' Traditional Shaker tune in the handwriting of Aaron Copland

Peter Pears with Julian Bream, Great Glemham House, during the tenth Aldeburgh Festival (17 June 1957, Morley Quatercentenary Concert)

The Dowager Countess of Cranbrook

Well, Peter dear, 72 or 75, not much in it! Being in the ranks of Festival OAPs and marvelling at all that has been achieved over the years, I still cherish above all those really early Jubilee times – with superb Albert, with terrifying Peter Quint from behind a gauze curtain, the fun for me and the family in *Let's Make*, you and Julian in the drawing room at Glemham – it's endless. I am so grateful and privileged to have been drawn into it all.

Lots more birthdays please and so much love.

FIDELITY

Joan Cross

As I write, dear Peter, the radio is offering the Overture to *The Bartered Bride* and I am at once back in Wimbledon during the gruelling wartime tour which found us (the Sadler's Wells Opera) in the theatre there at the height of the flying-bomb raids. We were presenting a matinée of this piece and there had already been a delay in raising the curtain because one vital member of the orchestra had been held up by a bomb on the railway. He had eventually arrived and Act I was well under way with Vašek (you), vital to Act II, not yet in the theatre. I found myself at the stage door frantically scanning the horizon. Just at the point of deciding that the audience would have to have their money back and go home, you rounded a corner a hundred yards away, weaving your way down the street at a snail's pace, gazing anxiously skywards, oblivious of the crisis on stage! There is still a generation of opera-goers who remember this wartime *Bartered Bride* and your enchanting performance which so enhanced the reputation of the Company.

Strange that at least two of the music staff of that time (1943) had doubts about offering you a contract, convinced that the voice was not operatic material! I, on the other hand, felt equally convinced that you would prove more than valuable. I'm glad I overruled my colleagues; I'm glad I was there to hear and see you as Almaviva in *The Barber*, Tamino in *The Flute*, Armand (so elegant) in *Traviata* and then Ferrando in *Così*.

After all this came *Peter Grimes*. But everyone knows about that saga! So, it merely remains for me to record that I feel privileged that I can still remember with such pleasure those unique occasions, some of which I shared with you, in (might we say?) roles that you never had time to repeat . . . simply because of the ultimate and inevitable Ben.

Salutations!

JOAN

Gordon Crosse

'The Frog Prince' from *The Cool Web* (1974).Words by Stevie Smith.
Autograph manuscript

Eric Crozier

A DAY OUT WITH BEN

My dear Peter,

This is part of a letter that I wrote to Nancy from Aldeburgh only a week or so after Ben had returned from his first visit with you to Venice.

20 February 1949

Yesterday Ben and I had the pleasantest day that I have enjoyed for several weeks. Both of us have been butting our heads against problems that were not to be solved by straining so much as by relaxation, though we could not admit the fact. Saturday morning was bright with sunshine, and crocuses and snow-drops looked very happy in the garden. Doctor Acheson came to visit Ben, and the three of us sat talking for an hour about the ills of the world and its stupidities – most reassuring conversation! And then we decided to set off in the car, taking sandwiches and cake and a bottle of beer each for lunch.

We drove north past Southwold to Covehithe, scrambled down to the deserted beach and sat at the water's edge to eat our lunch. After, we walked till we could see Lowestoft plain in the distance, then collected our things and drove gently back to Ferry Road at Southwold, where I packed all my luggage and said a temporary farewell to the little house. But before leaving altogether, we bicycled down to the river and across the common in the light of a magnificent sunset, and took tea at the Dutch Barn. Then, calling at the bookshop in the High Street, where Ben bought me a wonderful four-volume edition of the *Letters of Edward Fitzgerald*, across country to Iken, where we had been expected for tea and arrived for dinner. Margery Spring Rice, Cecil and Martin (her daughter and son-in-law) and their children and Arthur Oldham were there, and a very pleasant and cheerful evening it was until about eleven, when we drove back to Aldeburgh through a dark night with no moon but positively radiant with stars. It was midnight as we put the car away, and Orion was sinking down to the horizon. We boiled some milk and retired to bed with a mugful each.

Today is raw and misty, but we both feel in better heart for our day's holiday, when, for the first time this week, we were able to discuss our various problems and talk quite freely and idly about a dozen things – the new opera [*Billy Budd*], old operas, music, people, and the future. Now it is Sunday morning, the church bells are ringing, Ben is buried in his *Spring Symphony*, and I am standing in my bedroom writing this on the dressing-table top. Eleven o'clock is striking, and I can hear Ben at the piano downstairs. . . .

ERIC

Hugues Cuénod

To know Peter is to stand at an open window after hours in a stuffy room, and to feel fresh air in one's lungs and to see a lovely country of hills and vales and pastures and running waters, all this with a very kind and benevolent sun pouring on the lot. A sentiment of security as few people can project. Dear Peter, have many more years of radiating your intelligent kindness on all of us, your friends and admirers.

HUGUES

David Drew

TRIAD — WITH LYDIAN FOURTH

A

A dream, dreamt many years ago, in which every dimension of imaginable reality was in its proper place, although reality itself had provided no pretext or preparation for it; a dream so simple, rational, and lifelike that it would have been forgotten on waking if the conversation it consisted of had been elsewhere than in the Red House (which I had never visited) and with B and P (whom I had never met). Tea was served, time was most pleasantly passed, and I almost missed the train home. (Even in reality, there were still trains to be missed at Aldeburgh.) Someone had said there was ample time. But there wasn't. There seldom is.

C#

Several years later, another dream – almost identical with the first, except that instead of the awe-struck moment as I entered the room there was a delighted sense that it was my second visit, and the flattering discovery that my hosts recalled the previous one. How strange, I thought to myself, that they too had dreamt of it.

A + C#

To these remote yet still crystalline resonances of bells that were never actually to ring in what we call the 'real' world, there was recently added . . .

D#

A nightmare? Perhaps, but of a sort so often experienced that the novelty of finding myself in the role of an opera singer – incorrigible non-singer that I am – was preferable to the umpteenth replay of that arcane examination for which no stroke of work has been done. Waiting impatiently in the least favoured of Covent Garden's backstage dressing rooms, I wondered why I was about to make my long-awaited opera début wearing a sou'wester and oilskin from my distant past, and how on earth I could have failed to attend any rehearsals or even to enquire what the opera was. As no one was to be seen in the adjacent rooms or in the corridors, I rushed on stage and found that it was the deck of the HMS *Indomitable*. The performance had (of course) already begun. But there was no sign of Captain Vere or his crew, and no sound of music; just a milling throng, in which, abjectly, I tried to conceal myself. Detected by a spotlight, I knew that some kind of ensemble was about to begin and that I was expected to take part in it. At that moment, the first note of music welled up from the invisible orchestra pit, and instantaneously resolved nonsense into sense and nightmare into . . .

E

The clearest of dreams; from somewhere close by, there came the familiar but disembodied voice of an incomparable artist, singing, precisely as I had first and so often heard him and with that selfsame unsurpassable phrasing, 'Now the Great Bear and Pleiades. . . . ' In these lucidly dreamt moments, as in the vividness of reality, the clouds of human grief were indeed drawn up, and the lot of those of us who have not yet discovered our proper roles, and would surely fail to rehearse them adequately if we did, seemed more than merely tolerable.

Bettina Ehrlich

My dear Angelvoice,

This is a very special letter as it is for your 75th birthday and on top of that it is to be printed. So, instead of painting a picture for you in colours I have to paint one in words.

You know how foolish it would be if I tried to write about you as a musician. May it suffice to show how I feel about that by addressing you as I have done for years: dear Angelvoice.

Now I want to paint a little portrait of you as an art lover and collector. For in thirty-six years of living with Georg and eighteen years as administrator of his work after his death I have met a good many, but none – no, not one – like you. So, here comes the picture. . . .

One day you came to talk to Georg about something – I cannot remember what – and while crossing his large studio to greet him you patted a bronze, a little boy in a hooded cloak carrying a stick in his hand. You hardly looked at him. Yet, as I left you and Georg, I knew you would not leave the house without this child.

Nor did you. For when, later, you came downstairs you held it in your hands and you said to me: 'I am taking this with me.' And declining my offer to pack it, you opened a small suitcase you had deposited on the ground floor and wrapped the hooded child in a navy blue pullover (the only contents of the case!). Then, explaining that you had to hurry, you left. Not in a car, but walking at great speed, apparently quite indifferent to the weight of your new love.

That is how you always acquired Georg's works, man and beast alike. There never seemed to be an intention; it was a sudden falling in love – with the irresistible desire of immediate possession.

In this manner – without the conventional pondering, choosing, asking about cast numbers and other owners of previous casts – you built up, together with Ben, the biggest collection of Ehrlich bronzes that exists anywhere in the world.

When in 1964 Georg read your introduction to the catalogue of the Arts Council's touring exhibition of his bronzes which opened in the garden of the Red House, he said: 'Peter understands what I want to express in my work better than all the art historians and art critics who have written about me!'
Happy birthday, Angelvoice, and God bless you!

BETTINA

Georg Ehrlich: *Little Hooded Boy with a Stick* (1960) (bronze; height, 35 cms)

Osian Ellis

My dear Peter,

I have been trying to recall where and how we first met. It must have been at Westminster Cathedral when you and Ben came to listen to *A Ceremony of Carols* given by George Malcolm and his choirboys on the first Sunday in 1959. Ben wanted to hear the choir at close quarters with a view to writing a piece for them – in due course the delightful *Missa Brevis* materialized. Much later I came to appreciate his uncanny gift of writing for singers and instrumentalists: he would study and assimilate their particular 'properties', and not only would he compose for them works that displayed their virtues but he would also utilize their idiosyncrasies to fine effect.

After our performance of the *Ceremony* we were ushered into a vestry at the rear of the Cathedral and introduced to the newly appointed Cardinal. I was astonished to see busy young priests ministering to our needs bearing trays of cocktails – in chapel, and on a Sunday too! But all those amazements were overshadowed by the joy and pleasure of meeting you and Ben for the first time. I was touched by your friendly consideration towards a young musician, for you were already a legendary figure in the world of music whom I had admired from afar. I can still recall the exhilaration of a 30-year-old wending his way home that evening and virtually walking on air.

Later in 1959 I joined you in a Festival Hall performance, followed by the recording of Ben's exquisite *Nocturne* written a year earlier. This, surely, must be among the greatest of all settings of English poetry – always fresh and illuminating. Then in 1960 I was excited to be invited to play in the new opera, *A Midsummer Night's Dream* at Aldeburgh. It proved to be more exciting than I had anticipated: my colleague on the second harp was taken ill on the day of the dress rehearsal, and from then on I had to play both parts on one harp. During that first season you played Flute; I particularly enjoyed accompanying you during the Rustics' opera where you had to sing as Thisbe, *timidamente*, off-key. I'm sure that Ben was having a little dig at tenor tonality!

There were memorable tours abroad too with the *Dream*. I remember the beautiful – but cramped – baroque theatre at Schwetzingen with its delightful Schloss Park where some of our colleagues romped. At the Lion Inn opposite you introduced me to the barbaric Anglo-Saxon/Teutonic custom of eating raw meat. Mind you, I must admit that I have since succumbed to the succulence of Beefsteak Tartare – even at home.

Our sojourn of several days at the newly opened Coventry Cathedral comes to mind as we prepared and performed the *War Requiem* in 1962. At some quiet moment before the first performance I innocently observed to Ben how wonderful the work was, and he replied rather diffidently: 'Do you really think so?' I wondered at his apparent unease, but I slowly came to realize what agonies and frustrations he must have suffered during rehearsals with such large forces. What he heard from us, the performers, could not possibly match his musical conception. He was happy working with smaller forces, with people whom he knew. He called us by our first names – not only that, he would remember the names of our wives and children. I always found him full of warmth and humanity and, at appropriate times, a fine sense of humour. He was also extremely practical; even when he was ill and we were off on tour to the Continent, he would always enquire if we had everything we need – passports, music, money, etc.

I have a confession! Do you remember when you fell ill at our home? We told you your temperature was 100.5°; well, it wasn't: it was actually 105°. I do hope you will forgive this sin. A second thermometer confirmed this; our doctor could not believe it and rushed over at once while we covered you with ice. Later that night you dropped to 95° and we had to surround you with hot-water bottles. You will be pleased to know that Rene thought you were the most polite and considerate patient that she could have looked after.

But I must cease my gossiping. Dear Peter, thank you for recruiting me as an accompanist on so many concert tours and records, and for inspiring Ben and other composers to enhance the harp repertoire with lots and lots of new works for voice and harp. These are already being passed on to new generations of singers and harpists. I owe you a debt of gratitude also for the privilege of basking in the glow of your musicianship and experience, and for the pleasure of sharing your scintillating company as we travelled widely making new friends everywhere. There were many exciting occasions, and some amusing ones too. I recall my embarrassment, and your amusement, when an immigration officer at Harwich studied your passport and quizzically observed: 'Hmm . . . Peter Pears, Singer . . . I'm afraid I only know of Donald Peers!'

Happy Birthday . . .

Yours ever,

OSIAN

John Evans

Dear Peter,

It is not until one finishes one's formal education that one realizes that there is so much more to learn from relationships and the knowledge and experience of those we admire. During the past six years, while I have worked for you in various capacities, for the Festival, the Britten–Pears School and the Estate, I have learned so much from you about music, about art, about life itself. Most of our conversations seem, as I recall, to have taken place during our various travels – to Finland, Geneva, New York and Boston – though, more often than not, on our frequent (!) drives up and down the A12 between London and Aldeburgh. I also recall my first taste of lobster at the Vaakuna in Helsinki and our visit to the Frick Collection in New York and the impact of Bellini's *Saint Francis in Ecstasy* and El Greco's *Saint Jerome*. Taking notes for you as you advised conductor and soloists at the rehearsals for *War Requiem* in Boston in March last year was a privilege and something to be remembered always.

One of our more formal discussions was about *Death in Venice*, an edited and annotated transcript of which I included as an appendix to my Ph.D. thesis on the opera. I would like to recall here one detail from our discussion that illustrates the profound effect you and your great artistry had on Britten's creative impulse.

The interior monologues that articulate the structure of *Death in Venice*, that lend an insight into the intellectual and spiritual turmoil suffered by Aschenbach, were originally intended by Britten to be spoken. As Myfanwy Piper has written:

From several points of view [Britten] would have liked to have these passages spoken. It would have underlined the dryness and the isolation of this incorrigible writer; it would have provided a rest from singing for Aschenbach and it would done what we had in mind to do at the outset, create a music-drama in which speech, music and dance all had an integral place . . .

The composition sketch for *Death in Venice* occupied Britten from December 1971 to December 1972, a period that coincided with the Schütz Tercentenary Year, marked by a series of concerts in which you were the principal artist, singing the Evangelist in *The Christmas Story*, the *St Matthew Passion* and *The Resurrection Story*. Britten attended a number of these performances (and doubtless heard you preparing for them) and was reminded of the special

John Piper

Sketch for the Setting of Britten's 'Death in Venice' (1972)
(line and wash; 37.8 × 30.5cms)

quality you brought to the Evangelists' recitatives. He seized on the idea of making the interior monologues in *Death in Venice* freely articulated recitatives rather than spoken monologues, and decided to notate the *Death in Venice* recitatives as Schütz had notated his – with the pitch defined but the rhythm undefined. The melodic shape of the recitatives was notated by Britten from the natural verbal inflections that you gave to Myfanwy Piper's texts as you read them. He then left it to you (and to future Aschenbachs) to shape and articulate these monologues naturally and rhythmically, though lyrically and freely.

This is but one small instance in which your interpretative genius stimulated Britten's creative genius. What a lot we have to be grateful to you for, Peter, and how grateful Britten himself must have been.

With love, admiration and gratitude,

JOHN

Nancy Evans

Dearest Peter,

Some of the nicest things about growing older, it seems to me, are the clear memories and impressions of many years ago. In 1938 I was excited and happy to be a member of the Glyndebourne chorus, with the opportunity of learning so much from the partnership of Fritz Busch and Carl Ebert, in beautiful surroundings (it was my first real taste of the country, having grown up in Liverpool), and being made aware of the standard of perfection required of us; an ideal experience for a young singer.

Among the male chorus members, who were mainly Welsh, straight from the valleys – and a glorious sound they made – were three others, one Italian and two Englishmen, one of whom was very different physically from his Celtic colleagues. He was tall, fair-haired, reserved and poetic-looking.

I was too shy to talk to him much. He was Ebert's obvious choice for the Ghost of Il Re Duncano in Verdi's *Macbeth*, and that scene remains vividly in my mind. Ebert produced us all as individual characters, and in *Don Pasquale* the main chorus scene was encored at each performance. I am sure you remember what fun that was to do!

Our next meeting was not until 1946, the year when Ben and his music became part of my life: since then, your performances of his music, of Schubert and Bach and so much else have given us all a living standard to hand on to our young singers. The performances of the *St Matthew Passion* at Rotterdam and Amsterdam and subsequently in Aldeburgh Parish Church are highlights in my memory. I hear your Evangelist whenever I look at the Bach scores.

Impossible as it is to choose, I can only say that your Albert is very close to my heart, and in your recording of *Death in Venice* the subtlety and pacing of the near-recitative and the sensitive response to the words show supreme artistry.

How lucky I am, darling Peter, to have the joy of working, talking and laughing with you and with all the talented young singers who are drawn to our lovely school through the power of the creative genius of Ben and Peter.

With abiding love and admiration,

NANCY

Faber Music Limited

The Directors of Faber Music offer their most distinguished colleague a *fortissimo* message of congratulation and good wishes on his 75th Birthday. They are the more happy to do this since 1985 marks twenty years of music publishing at Faber; it has been a great encouragement in our formative years to have had the patronage and wise guidance of an experienced and learned elder whose eminence and supreme artistry are universally recognized. Benjamin Britten was one of our Founding Directors and it is a rare privilege now to have Peter Pears as a colleague on the board. Every member of the staff feels honoured by this association and joins with us in sending a birthday greeting.

DONALD MITCHELL	PATRICK CARNEGY	PETER DU SAUTOY
MARTIN KINGSBURY	SALLY CAVENDER	PIERS HEMBRY
RODERICK BISS	GILES DE LA MARE	TONY POCOCK

Peter Pears with Kathleen Ferrier, Edinburgh Festival, September 1947. 'Two of the people who helped to make the Edinburgh three-week Festival a success. Peter Pears, tenor, and Kathleen Ferrier, contralto, take a stroll through Princes Street Gardens.'

Dietrich Fischer-Dieskau

My dear Peter,

wenn irgend jemand unter den Musikern, die mir begegnet sind, als Vorbild genannt werden sollte, so würde ich nicht zögern, Deinen Namen zu nennen. Seit dem Tage, an dem wir uns zur Uraufführung des *War Requiem* trafen, bist Du mir immer als der Aristokrat unter den Sängern erschienen: Geistbestimmt, phantasievoll, von erlesenem Geschmack geleitet und untadelig in der musikalischen Leistung. Wer kann schon von sich behaupten, er hätte einem Genius wie Benjamin Britten schöpferische Anregung und wählenden Impuls bei den Sujets gegeben?

Das Zusammenwirken mit Dir zählt zu den wichtigsten Elementen in meinem Leben, das an wesentlichen Begegnungen nicht gerade arm gewesen ist. Aber eben – Menschlichkeit und künstlerische Grösse gehen selten eine solche Symbiose ein wie bei Dir. Älter zu werden, gibt der Erinnerung neue und wichtigere Funktion. Denke ich an Dich und Ben, wird's mir warm ums Herz. Darum immer wieder Dank und die herzlichsten Wünsche.

Yours ever,

DIETER

[If someone were to ask whom I'd choose as a paragon among the musicians I know, I would not hesitate to mention your name. Since the day when we met at the time of the first performance of the *War Requiem*, you have always seemed to me the aristocrat among singers: of rare intelligence, highly imaginative, with infallible taste and irreproachable in performance. Who else can claim that he has inspired a genius like Benjamin Britten with the creative stimulus and choice of subjects to compose so many works specially for him?

I count the experience of working with you among the most important ingredients in a life that has not been poor in significant encounters. But beyond that, such a fusion of humanity and artistic greatness as yours is rare indeed. When one grows older recollection acquires a new and more important function. I have only to think of you and Ben for it to warm my heart. For that I send you as always my thanks and affectionate greetings.]

Jill Gomez

I shall never forget the morning when Jack Phipps, my agent at that time, rang to ask if I would sing the Governess in *The Turn of the Screw* with Peter Pears as Quint. I had known Britten's operas through recordings ever since I'd arrived in England from Trinidad some years before as a schoolgirl and been galvanized by them and the haunting singing of Peter Pears, not least that moment of stillness and pain as his voice pierced one to the heart: 'Now the Great Bear and Pleiades . . . Who can turn skies back and begin again?' It seemed unbelievable that this was now 1973 and that I would shortly be singing the Governess alongside the Quint of Peter Pears, the role's creator, in what was to turn out to be the last run of performances that he and the English Opera Group ever gave together.

To be sure I had already sung the First Niece in the historic BBC Television production of *Peter Grimes*, filmed and recorded simultaneously in the Maltings in 1969. At that time Peter – and Ben, miles away in front of the orchestra – were august presences to whom a young singer would never have dared to speak. But here I was, in Colin Graham's famous production at Sadler's Wells Theatre, battling for the soul of the poor terrified little Miles and wondering how it was that Quint, with his irresistible vocal allure, was not the undisputed victor.

Learning the Governess was one of the strangest and most terrifying periods of study I have ever experienced. I steeped myself in Henry James's story – whose style I must confess often taxed my patience – but while it was one thing as a reader to marvel at James's slow and almost evasive narrative right up to the ghastly sudden climax of the child's death, it was quite another to hear Britten's version, which deeply disturbed me from the first note. I found myself fighting the need to give in and become submerged in the story, of whose true horror I had become aware only through the music. I knew I had to do this before I could attain the necessary sense of detachment to decide how I could play the role.

I suppose that all sopranos who have sung the role must go through a very jumpy state during rehearsals, a feeling compounded by the difficulty of much of the music. At one such moment during the dress rehearsal, and at the ominous words 'Lost in my labyrinth' I did indeed get hopelessly lost, owing to the scurrying groups of semiquaver triplets going on in the orchestra under the Governess's frozen but breathlessly fast 3/8 vocal line. I had just wound my way down the curved staircase, clinging to the banister for support, and was standing disconsolately on the bottom step, waiting for the conductor's signal to try it again, when out of the corner of my eye I caught sight of someone standing in the wings, beckoning to me. I involuntarily caught my breath because unless the Governess and I were hallucinating together, I had just seen the ghost of the composer of the piece.

Ben had not been expected at the rehearsal; indeed we had not seen him at all over the whole rehearsal period of that late summer of 1973 as he was by then so very ill. But here he actually was, leaning heavily upon a stick and calling to me. Much to the conductor Kenneth Montgomery's surprise, instead of continuing back up the stairs I slowly, and as though in a trance, walked across the stage and into the wings. 'Hello, I'm Benjamin Britten,' whispered the ghost, with his free hand taking mine, and without further ado talked to me about how the problems in the aria might best be overcome. If I remember correctly, one of his hints was not to sing it out too much, but almost to whisper the words and to beware at the third quaver in each bar, which tended to get stuck, thereby interfering with the rhythmic flow. I thanked him profusely and, still feeling I was dreaming, drifted back on to the stage where, with the benefit of the composer's advice, the aria went perfectly for the first time since rehearsals had begun.

I never saw Ben again – he just disappeared. But I know I didn't imagine this scene, if only because on the first night I received a personal telegram from him saying how much he'd enjoyed the dress rehearsals and wishing me luck. On all my subsequent Britten first nights, whether as the Governess or Tytania, a telegram would come from the Red House, and at Christmas there was always a card with a message.

I have often reflected how incredibly fortunate I have been to have touched – and been touched by – the era of Britten and Pears. So much of my career has been to do with singing Ben's music that it seems only right that one of the greatest debts I gratefully acknowledge is the lasting inspiration of once having shared a stage with the legendary Peter's Quint.

Colin Graham

Dearest Peter,

Happy Birthday!

I wish I could be with you at Snape on this very auspicious occasion but life has drawn us geographically apart and made it impossible. Drawn apart, but not so far that memories of the things we did together at Snape with Ben do not still fill me with the most excited kind of nostalgia. They are memories of things that have enriched my life beyond measure: they will never be forgotten and I shall be eternally thankful for them.

To name but three of the hundreds (one for each of your magnificent twenty-five years!):

Idomeneo: your performance, Ben's performance (both unequalled by any I have heard since), the fire, the miracle of the Blythburgh performances and the miracle of the phoenix at Snape.

You and Ben and *Gerontius* – I was only in the audience, but this experience sums up all that was good and wonderful in the non-operatic, triumphant happenings in the Golden Days of Snape.

Last and greatest: Aschenbach! I still wonder at the extraordinary affinity between you, Ben, Mann, Aschenbach, in any combination you care to fancy. At your amazing feat of rehearsing it for the first time with Ben undergoing his operation – all hearts in all mouths as you assumed that role of Lear-like proportions. That first night at Snape – and Ben's first night later on when he saw and heard it for the first time – all hearts in all mouths again!

There are so many things to remember and share with you: Venice with you both during the writing of *Curlew* and others – my visits to the Red House before I lived in Orford: the walks on the golf course and by the ferry at Orford when so many momentous things were conceived and discussed – including life – so many things in those thirty-two years. How time draws things together and remembers all the good and great things while obliterating anything remotely unsatisfactory!

Above them all hang the memory of Ben and all he meant (and means) and the present and past glories of Snape where you will be tonight and I will not: even if I cannot share them with you tonight, they will always be there.

With love –

COLIN

39

Vlado Habunek

Dearest Peter,

At the thought of your birthday I am overwhelmed by a swarm of sound, pictures, moods with you in the centre, in different places, at different times, coming and disappearing like the revolving beam of a lighthouse bringing back with each flash another of those exquisite moments. London, Aldeburgh, New York, Paris, Dubrovnik, Zagreb, Montreal, Amsterdam, Venice. Your unforgettable recital in Zagreb on your way to the Far East, talk of the Noh plays you were going to see, which ended in your and Ben's masterpiece. The Palazzo Mocenigo while you were working on it. Embarrassing situation with that silly New York conductor. I wonder whether you remember our sitting in the middle of a big open square in Montreal so that Ben would not catch us discussing the proposal for an 'arranged' score of *Curlew River*. Your comforting look when later on, during a Christmas dinner at Marion's Aldeburgh place, Ben got angry about an American review that I thought was a rave. The time I found you rushing down the steep steps of Fort Lovrjenac in Dubrovnik in the middle of a rehearsal of *Lucretia*, and Ben saying: 'We shall remain friends but I don't *see* what you have done. I only *hear*. And what I hear I can't stand.' Without you and Marion I would have probably jumped into the sea from the top of the fortress. A wonderful evening another time in Dubrovnik when Ben could not conduct, so we brought in Alex Gibson. After what must have been *Les Illuminations*, Ben consented to forget his arm in the sling in order to accompany you in a few songs on the piano. I can still see the faces of the audience and the musicians listening in sheer rapture. Your triumphs in New York. Alice Tully audience bewitched. The Met, becoming with you a completely different place: musicianship, elegance and grand air, putting to shame the operatic ostentation. An infinitely sad moment late one night in front of the Mayflower Hotel: New York at your feet and Ben alone ill at home. At other times so much fun with you and Ben, for instance your stratagems to hold at bay unwanted admirers or mischievously reverse the situation like the famous Dubrovnik 'Let's be kind to So-and-so!' (The three-syllable 'So-and-so' might read this, so I can't involve you even if you don't remember the name.) Your masterclass in Aldeburgh. One after another of the young singers putting all their heart into a Bach phrase. At the end, with uncanny simplicity, you doing it for them with a shattering effect. I was able to stay at Aldeburgh only a very short time, but I was glad to be as soon as possible alone with that phrase.

I could go on and on, without mentioning your recordings when far from you. You see how much your art, your presence, your friendship have done for me alone. How many are those all over the world whose life you have enriched!

Thank you, dearest Peter,

VLADO

The Earl of Harewood

My dear Peter,

I am sitting in an aeroplane trying to make up my mind why you have always impressed me as one of the greatest singers I ever heard and then wondering how to express it without repeating what's been said umpteen times before. Virtually each one of the very many performances I heard you give produced the sort of total pleasure to which that splashy adjective 'great' is too often attached and there must be a common denominator somewhere.

Was it that extraordinary attack and rhythmical precision – I think of 'Sì come nella penna', the first thing I ever heard you sing (on a gramophone record)? Was it what it would be inadequate to call your diction, that extremely positive and delicate use of words – 'Since she whom I loved hath paid her last debt'? Was it that wonderful *legato* line and discriminating use of *portamento* – 'I wonder as I wander', your performance of which in Ben's arrangement is the saddest lack amongst your gramophone recordings? Was it your indefatigable search for new material (new I mean to most of us) which first brought Schütz and 'Beata viscera' to Aldeburgh?

It's hard to pin down, but I remember that once when we were talking about singers you said that you thought a lack of imagination, not shortage of technique, was what kept most of them from achieving what they set out towards, and I have often thought about that since. It's that quality one remembers about particular singing performances, not the golden (or the silvery or even the brazen) sounds, but the way they were deployed to bring the composer's intentions, or maybe just the artist's aims, to the listener.

I first heard you on a gramophone record of the *Michelangelo Sonnets* more than forty years ago and then not long afterwards as Tamino with touring Sadler's Wells. You always had a highly individual, immediately recognizable sound, but even your admirers could have been forgiven astonishment as well as gratification at the way you dominated the big apparatus of *Peter Grimes* when Sadler's Wells reopened after the war. All the same, what has haunted the memory ever since was not the remarkable size of your performance but the unique sound quality of the reiterated 'Who . . . who . . .' in the pub scene – not just soft singing as every other Grimes has attempted but something much deeper, at the same time full of tragedy, because so filled with understanding, and not without hope; scene-stopping, because so purely beautiful, and moving the drama forward, because one could not wait to know what would come next. Erwin Stein used to say that one of the marks of the interpreter was for the listener to sense the precise duration of a sustained note as soon as it began. Imagination, you are right, not technique!

Yours ever,

GEORGE

Heather Harper

Dear Peter,

You will probably never have guessed that as well as being your devoted colleague I have been also your devoted fan for a long time.

It all started when you and Ben came to my home town of Belfast to give a recital at Queen's University.

I was a schoolgirl then, very shy, but I managed to pluck up enough courage to come backstage afterwards to ask you both for your autographs.

I could not have imagined in my wildest dreams that one day we would be singing together at the world première of *War Requiem* with Ben conducting.

Later on we were to sing opera together and share recitals at the Maltings with Ben accompanying.

These occasions have been highlights in my career, which I treasure deeply.

You are an exemplary musician and a model for others to follow, having set such high standards throughout your career.

I would like to add my warmest birthday greetings to the many tributes that you will receive.

Happy Birthday, Peter,

HEATHER

Hans Werner Henze

Chamber Music I (1958): Section VIII, 'Möcht ich ein Komet sein', bars 17–30 Autograph manuscript

HRH The Princess of Hesse and the Rhine

EXTRACT FROM A LETTER HOME WRITTEN BY PEG ON THE FAR EASTERN
JOURNEY OF LUPEG AND BENPET

Japan   23 February 1956

By the time we reached Kyoto (7½ hours from Tokyo) it was snowing hard and
very cold. In Kyoto we stayed in a Japanese inn. At the entrance to the inn,
which was hidden away in a plain little street lined with wooden walls of other
houses, all the maids in kimonos greeted us with deep bows – kneeling on the
ground and touching the floor with their heads, we all took off our shoes at the
door and, feeling over-lifesize and rather British, we flapped along the polished
floors to our rooms. All doors (and most of the walls *are* doors) slide and people
pop in and out at any corner of the room and you never feel alone, you can't lock
anything. At our room door off come the slippers and one then walks about in
stockinged feet. Our room consisted of two small rooms, a little porch, a minute
garden and a washroom and a more than unusual and complicated lavatory –
everything spotlessly clean.

At night our beds replaced the red lacquer table – quilts to lie on and quilts to
cover you. We were all rather cold and a bit overcome till we were given sake
(hot rice wine) in great quantities. Our gentle maids never left our sides and
tried to read in our eyes our next wish. Ben (who is the most conservative of the
lot) looked worried and like a wet depressed dog, he could find nowhere for his
long legs and was cold and worried by the kimono he was made to wear! But we
all cheered up after we had had boiling hot baths (and I mean boiling! we nearly
had heart attacks as a result). I was made to go first by the men. The maid
undressed me and led me to the bathrooms. One room for soaping and getting
off the soap and the other for the bath (built in) and meditation. I didn't do
much of the latter and I was nearly steamed alive. Maid put me into clean cotton
kimono and covered me up with a beautiful warm silk kimono on top, took me
back to our room and gave me tea out of beautiful pottery mugs.

Never can I describe how we four laughed at this time. We really became
hysterical and Ben, Lu and Peter were so funny and looked so odd my sides
ached from laughing, and my legs ached from kneeling the entire time.

We spent an evening in a Japanese family – flower-arranging and a shorter tea
ceremony being part of our entertainment, aria from *Tosca*!! and flute solo by
the children! being further entertainment. Ben and Peter accompanied the
children. We all sang 'Three blind mice' together – liked our new friends

'Kumergai' (owner of a *beautiful* paper shop) but hated press who flash-lighted and tape-recorded the entire time.

We returned to Tokyo on Thursday 16th, and were plunged into the Tokyo tempo. Ben and Peter busy with rehearsals for Ben's orchestral concert – not easy playing with Japanese orchestra, though they were good. Ben always in demand – Japanese are doing *Peter Grimes* and want to do *Turn of the Screw* – press and broadcasts nearly drove them mad. Their second televised concert a huge success.

Sinfonia da Requiem, Les Illuminations – Peter singing, a great success – he is so glad to be out of the tropics – *no* good for vocal chords. *Young Person's Guide to the Orchestra.*

We all thoroughly enjoyed the Kabuki plays. Ben and Peter fascinated – they are something very moving and remarkable.

Wolfsgarten

Dearest Peter,

This is only one of the many recollections of experiences we have shared, which have enriched and continue to enrich my life.

Love,

PEG   X

45

Derek Hill

Music for a Princess (oils 21 X 25 cms). An Aldeburgh Festival exhibit 1982. Malkin Safe 22, 23 and Liverton 9 and both above the

Barbara Holmes

My Dearest Cousin,

Love, congratulations and homage to you on your 75th birthday! You are truly my dearest cousin; we have had so much in common besides just blood. Do you remember when you came to spend your holidays with us at Dadbrook? We were both about 10, and I was so impressed and a bit envious of you when you played a piece called 'Vesperale' by Easthope Martin so fluently. And I ambitiously, and painfully unsuccessfully, struggled with Rachmaninov's C sharp minor Prelude. (I had to leave out the fast bit in the middle!)

Poor us, we were both orphans of Empire, though your spell of separation was longer than mine. We must have been scarred by the First World War and that separation.

I wish I'd seen more of you when we were growing up – those early days in London. We'd both set foot on our musical paths, but from the beginning I was never in the same class. You never chased after 'the bitch goddess success', you were too good a musician ever to be tempted by vanity. We had some good times together, though. Do you remember when you and Ben and I gave a concert in the Master's Lodge in Balliol? I remember, in the ante-room before we started, your singing a note through your nose – *meeee*, and listening to the resonance. I was fascinated and thought, well, here is a true professional.

Later, once when you were staying with us at Charlbury Road you came into our bedroom one morning and Henry and I sat up in bed and watched you do your yoga exercises in your pyjamas. *Oooom!* Those were the good years when the great Britten–Pears partnership was being built up, *The Ascent of F6*, the night-club spell and so on.

When the day came when you and Ben departed for America we were so sad that you would be so far away, but tremendously admired your perception of the evil of war and your courage to have no part in it. Quaker blood. The other day I came across a letter you wrote to us from Amityville. You said in it you felt continuous anxiety about family and friends left in England, and greatly depressed over the whole senseless violence, which we know will never settle anything. However, out of those times came great music for which the whole musical world is grateful, and in this volume we all want to say thank you.

So may the sun shine on you always, and many congratulations on all you've achieved and all you've given musicians and music-lovers everywhere.

BARBIE

The Very Reverend Walter Hussey

Dear Peter,

I look back with gratitude for the many kindnesses and much inspiration you have brought to me since 1943. Very early on there was the time when I stood spellbound in the wings and heard you sing in *La Bohème*; there was the unforgettable experience of the first night of *Peter Grimes*; and that night in the Wigmore Hall when you sang the *Donne Sonnets*. I remember the occasion in S. Matthew's, Northampton, when I was so moved by your singing of 'Waft her, angels' from Handel's *Jephtha* that I very nearly forgot to turn over the page for Ben!

It was not only for these and countless other great musical occasions that I and many others think of you with gratitude. It was comparatively rarely that I had the pleasure of giving you hospitality for the night, but when that happened there was always plenty of laughter. Do you remember how we laughed when Ben was teasing Mrs Cotton, offering to accompany her and showing on the piano how he would supply the sound of bathwater dripping, when she suddenly said, quite naturally and utterly irrelevantly, 'What lovely hair you've got, Mr Britten'?

In many ways your voice seemed to grow ever better as the years passed. You once wrote on a card from New York, 'Not bad to be making one's début at the Met at 64!' Not bad indeed! Particularly when the début was a triumph.

Congratulations on your 75th birthday! I hope it is a very happy day, and may you have many more to come.

WALTER

Graham Johnson

Dearest Peter,

Like many musicians of the younger generation, I got to know you through your gramophone recordings. I was a teenager newly arrived from Rhodesia and the gramophone library in Porchester Road W2 was responsible for a large part of my delayed musical education! I discovered the music of Britten, and at the same time the art of Pears, much later than youngsters reared in this country. *Les Illuminations* was my first discographical revelation; in the relatively few minutes it took for you to reach the phrase *'Et je danse'*, where you moved magically up to an ethereal high B flat, I had become a fanatical admirer. For the first time I could say with Whitman:

> I hear not the volumes of sound merely,
> I am moved by the exquisite meanings.

I then got to know the operas, and everything else by Ben and after that your recordings of the great Schubert cycles and *Dichterliebe*. The Pears–Britten *Lieder* partnership was to change my life entirely for it was through you that I came to realize that I wanted to spend my life accompanying the song repertoire.

I know that you are not over-interested in listening to records yourself. (Ben in his Aspen speech had some cutting and wise things to say about music at the flick of a switch.) By the standards of some singers you have not recorded as much as you might if you had been in love with technology or ambitious for quantity rather than quality. I think you and Ben believed that recordings were meant simply to *preserve* what had worked well in the concert hall; they were not an end in themselves, a mere marketable means of 'filling in gaps in the catalogue'. This is why the issue of each of your discs has been an event worth waiting for. Each represents years of work and thought, in Matthew Arnold's words –

> Of Toil not sever'd from Tranquility, –
> Of Labour, that in still advance outgrows
> Far noisier schemes, accomplish'd in Repose,
> Too great haste, too high for Rivalry.

Many thousands of people have heard you in the flesh, a much smaller number has got to know you personally. The vast majority of your world-wide following of millions 'know' you only as I first did. But the extraordinary thing is that after being at various times your pupil, *répétiteur* and accompanist, I now realize that your manifold qualities as a man and artist are faithfully preserved and accounted for on the discs as I first heard them. I can truly say that I got to know *you* through your recordings. And in knowing you well there has not been a single let-down or disappointment, never a need to adjust my teenager's mental picture of what it would be like to meet you in real life: you were indeed as you sounded – patrician yet approachable, cultivated yet intuitive, serious yet great fun. The humanity I heard coming from my portable gramophone in my London bedsit in 1967 was the truth about you: you did not sing a word of a lie. You may argue that a great singer *can't* lie. Perhaps, but I know too many good ones who can.

It is only the rarest people who are what they do, and do what they are. If any of your fans on the other side of the world read this, I can assure them that in your case (rare in the world of recording 'takes' and double-takes) it *is* safe to trust the evidence of their ears: to love and admire you at a distance is not to love in vain.

Your devoted

GRAHAM

Hans Keller

Every musician knows that normally singers are amongst the most unmusicianly, if not indeed unmusical, members of our profession, a close second, of no further significance for the present article, being cellists. In this sense, Peter Pears is not a singer at all, for his musicality is profound and comprehensive, and his musicianship of such a rare quality that one can say without exaggeration that otherwise one encounters it only amongst composers, and leading composers at that. But then, one could describe Peter Pears as a composer too: great performance being the tail-end of composition, a great interpreter invariably evinces genuinely creative talent.

It must needs be a variable tail-end. Since the composer, by not completing the work himself, ensures the tail-end's variability, it follows as a matter of musico-logical course that no two performances by the same interpreter can possibly be identical, that his interpretation has to vary and grow from performance to performance. One had to hear Peter Pears in countless performances of the same work or role in order to realize how he created a new creative substance each time he realized the composer's own content.

Owing to the many operatic roles and extra-operatic parts that Britten composed with Pears's musical personality and voice in mind, and of which the latter gave so many overwhelming performances, the musician of today is not likely to be aware of the breadth of Pears's interpretative vision – and I am not only thinking of such other composers – for example, Schubert – whom the two have interpreted jointly, perhaps even on commercial disc.

Anybody who remembers Pears's stunning performances in, say, *The Bartered Bride* or *Così fan tutte* will agree that he brought to such works, or rather, such roles, the same re-creative intensity as to the music of Britten; in addition, there was, of course, his outstanding acting, which was always ruled by musical considerations – even under unmusical opera producers. In particular, I shall always remember, down to the subtlest phrasing detail, his – Ferrando's – deeply moving dominant-minor entries (yes, each of them was different) in the A major duet with Fiordiligi: in my lifetime, he has been the only performer with a deep insight into what the dominant minor meant to Mozart.

Altogether, then, Pears can realistically be ranked as one of the very few great interpreters of our time. Among all musicians, it is only performers whose musicality, ideally, has to be two-dimensional: their understanding has to be as profound as their creativity. Pears attained this ideal with such ease that one never heard him struggle with a part, an ease which produced, throughout his professional life, nothing but mastery. But then, inaudibly, he also met a negative condition of interpretative mastery: so far as I am aware (and I probably heard him more often than anybody alive), he never undertook any performing task without being sure of his exceptional insight into the music in question. At the same time, we didn't hear him in everything he wholly understood: for instance, he'd have loved to enact Tristan. Curiously enough, my mother once told me that the greatest Tristan she had ever heard (under Mahler) sounded, vocally and phrasingly, like Pears's twin brother.

Oliver Knussen

'The Valley Wind' (revised 1984) from *Three Chinese Lyrics* (1965). Words by Arthur Waley
Autograph manuscript

Bob and Doris Ling

Many Happy Returns of your birthday, dear Peter, and a big thank you for the fulfilment of the dream that you and Ben once had the courage to bring into being: the restoration of the old Maltings Building into the really famous Concert Hall it has become. To so many people, especially the youngsters, it is a place where they have an opportunity to listen and improve upon their love of music and the arts. To Bob and me it has meant a continuation of our young married life when our world was wrapped around this very place with the making of malt, and now because of an ideal dream of yours we are still lucky enough to spend our life within the very heart of it all.

In the early days of our working here we shared so many experiences with you but the one Bob most likes to recall is when on one winter afternoon we were spring cleaning the hall. Bob was after the cobwebs in the roof and I was on the foot of the ladder. You and Ben walked through the door. I jumped off the ladder to say hello and the ladder started to slip across the polished floor. Bob's voice as he shouted certainly didn't need amplification or special acoustics, as I remember!

We do so enjoy seeing you at concerts for, as with everyone, you are always so very nice to us. In fact Bob says the waiting in the courtyard doesn't seem the same when you aren't around. You must be very proud of all you have accomplished and your work and life must go into so many homes, for when the schoolchildren leave the hall from their tours clutching their programmes and their papers they are so full of it all it must spill all over when they arrive home.

A few weeks back we had two of the Decca boys for a weekend in Aldeburgh. They were sorry not to see you but I'm sure your ears must have burned, although you were far away, as we spent the time reminiscing of the days of yourself and Ben, John Culshaw, David Harvey, Jimmy Locke and Dave Frost, not forgetting Tony Steinman and dear old Wilkie, with you and Ben sitting on our small settee listening to the playbacks, and especially the times Bob and I joined you all for a relaxing drink after all was completed to your satisfaction. Although they have been gone so long and travelled so far you've only to hear the animation in their voices and brightness of their eyes to know that to them here will be always special.

Bob and I both wish you well, dear Peter, and send our love,

DORIS & BOB

54

Hans Ludwig

Venezia: Chiesa Il Redentore, Palladio
'This musical-architectural detail of Palladio's Il Redentore in Venice represents for me two parts in a fugue or two friends singing together in different registers. The one could be the bass, the other one the tenor. I hear the music, but cannot recognize the melody. I hope you can! It must be a hymn to you on your birthday.'   [H.L.]

Witold Lutoslawski

'Deuxième tapisserie' from *Paroles tissées* (1965). Autograph manuscript

Neil Mackie

My dear Peter,

Thursday, 25 April 1968, is a date to remember! I had been asked to prepare some of our favourite Rosseter songs for your masterclass at the Royal Scottish Academy of Music and Drama on that day and as a result of our first meeting I came south, gave up the idea of school teaching and began a career in singing. However, not only did you become my teacher but also my true friend and mentor.

There are so many memories and events to cherish since then . . . lessons at the Studio (often followed by dinner), an introduction to the music of Percy Grainger, our first Good Friday Passion and a subsequent Horham lunch, a Swiss holiday with Rita and Kathleen to include the wild flowers of Tarasp and sunstroke, a memorable visit to Wolfsgarten and an equally memorable *War Requiem*, the delightful sunsets at Savonlinna, a Polish trip and several intense conversations about your beloved Ben, thumbs down at Elmau, a Claydon concert followed by the hilarious and extraordinary journey to Ruislip, lunch at Hungerford and a 'Ben' lecture at Bridgwater. . . . The list is endless.

> Where love has been, there will always remain
> the echo of the song that it sings.

It gives me immense pleasure to salute you on your 75th birthday and I thank you for your friendship and affection over these happy years. Kathleen joins me in sending our fondest love and we look forward to many more of your visits to Ruislip.

Yours ever,

NEIL

PS   Lang may yer lum reek!

57

Hugh Maguire

My dear Peter,

May I wish you a Very Happy Birthday – not only from myself, but also to convey the greetings of our lovely school!

We all know and admire your great love and work for the cause of music, but not quite so many are aware of your affection for your garden and what grows therein, so forgive me if I draw a parallel . . . for here you are, three score years and fifteen, and, as with other great musicians of our time, the intellectual capacity continues to grow, but the mechanism to give voice to it begins to fail and falter and what is left is a rich 'compost' of musicianship to feed from. May I congratulate you, dear Peter, on your arrival at this ripe, fertile and mature state? You may think you had arrived before now, but no, only from today may you steam!

All your gardens are now well established. At the Red House those lovely plants and shrubs and lawns are encouraged to flourish, watched over by that splendid (forgive the pun) Irish Yew! Year after year we continue to admire the luscious and beautiful 'flowers' that abound from your Aldeburgh Festival, and now we can also follow the fortunes of the many 'seedlings' from our nursery at Snape, flourishing in the landscape of international music-making.

I remember as a young student, new to London, coming in contact with some of the greatest conductors of that period – Bruno Walter, Furtwängler, De Sabata, Koussevitzky, Toscanini, Monteux and Enesco. Many had been out of the public eye during the war and all were old and wise. They created an enormous impression on me and a big sensation with the concert-going public who were hungry for quality things.

The music that these musicians performed was sustained with rare poise – surprisingly so, coming as it did after those tormented years in the early forties – and one felt an unshakeable inner peace. Experience and wisdom are the product of accumulated years, and when one comes in contact with these qualities one is in touch with truth. The lucky students that know and are close to you are very privileged people indeed, because you have joined these exalted ranks . . . and you are still here – 'ex . . . cellently bright'!

However there is work to be done. New fashions and practices in sound production, particularly related to baroque and early classical music (not greatly to my liking) abound just now. It is almost a case of authenticity taking the place of musicality. We need the likes of you to guide us and put a steadying hand on such 'trends' and to show us how to rediscover the joys of our profession and allow us all, at our school, to reap the harvest of your long association with distinguished artists and to gather the fruits of your total devotion to our noble art.

We lift our glasses and salute you. ERGO BIBAMUS!

Affectionately,

HUGH

Peter Pears taking a masterclass on Gluck's *Le Cinesi* during the 1976 'Operatic Excerpts' Course for Singers at the Britten–Pears School for Advanced Musical Studies. The students are Hilary Straw (soprano) singing Sivene and Timothy German (tenor) singing Silango. The *répétiteur* is Roger Vignoles and the conductor Michael Lankester.

Lucie Manén

Among those of my pupils who became world famous Peter Pears stands out as the most senior, who, at an advanced age, had the courage to take up singing lessons with me after – as he wrote – 'not having worked with a teacher for a number of years and feeling the need for a good one'.

With enthusiasm and zest he studied with me like any youngster, ambitious and very much favoured by his natural artistic gifts and skills. No sooner had he mastered the grammar of my teaching, the attack of the tone from the *imposto*, to 'cantare con la gorga' on *esclamazione* (Caccini), than he was eager to try it out by himself before an audience. It was a success! 'You have given Peter a new lease of life,' said Ben to me over the telephone.

Soon after, in 1965, Ben wrote, 'It is a great thing for Peter that he has met you and worked with you, Lucie, it has added something considerable to his life. I feel I may be allowed to share in that "something" now too!' And he invited me to the Red House.

During the years to come Peter and I enjoyed very much working hard together to our mutual benefit, Peter always anxiously waiting for the next lesson, 'like Carpaccio's little dog', as he wrote to me once from Venice.

In September 1972 we opened a 'study week for singers' at Snape Maltings, the foundation stone of the Britten–Pears School. It was meant to become a training centre for singers and, as I myself very much hoped, a training college for prospective teachers, i.e. singers, who at the end of their career would be prepared to undergo a basic interdisciplinary training in anatomy, physiology, acoustics and psychology. 'The Need for Interdisciplinary Training of Singing Teachers' ought to be on the curriculum for all prospective singing teachers, to further the standard of our profession.

Unfortunately my ideas were not – not yet? – taken up at the Britten–Pears School. Yet looking back on so many years of teaching Peter Pears I feel grateful for being honoured, after his appearance at the Teatro la Fenice as Gustav von Aschenbach in *Death in Venice*, by a letter of appreciation and gratitude from him – most unusual in our hectic time. It reads:

How incredibly lucky I was to 'find' you just at the time when I most needed you, and how wonderfully understanding you have been to me for – how many years? It was all part of my 'destiny–fate–good fortune' that I should go to far-and-away the most intelligent teacher I had met just at the time when I was ripe enough to profit from her (and stand up to her!) – And just as I thank my stars for so many things, so I thank you, dear Lucie, for all your help, your kindness, your courage, your warmth, your generosity, the example that you set us all. *Death in Venice* is obviously the peak of my career, and it is marvellous to have you there with me, and Ben, up above the snow-line! (in Igls).

Colin Matthews

'Shadows in the Water' (1978–9). Words by Thomas Traherne. Autograph manuscript

Tony Mayer

One must have lived in England during the war – and particularly during the Blitz or the V1 or V2 period to realize of what metal the Britishers are made. One never really mentioned the bombings. It simply wasn't done. 'Rather noisy tonight,' said the taxi driver, sitting quite unruffled at the wheel while the bombs fell right and left. Caught under the rubble, a woman sipped patiently a 'lovely cup of tea'. 'Don't worry, dear, it'll be all right,' said she . . . and passed away. People groped their way in the blackout. The house shook but the party went on. The theatres were full. So were the all too rare concerts. At the National Gallery, devoid of its pictures – save *one*! – Myra Hess organized a marvellous series of lunchtime concerts. Peter and Ben performed there. On a more modest scale – with the enthusiastic assistance of my old friend Felix Aprahamian – I started a series of French Concerts, either at the Wigmore Hall or at St Peter's, Eaton Square. I remember one of those particularly well. It was a programme of early French music. Peter had just started singing an unaccompanied piece by Pérotin when suddenly the horrid, all too familiar buzzing of a V1 was heard. Nobody even batted an eyelid. Standing motionless in the choir, Peter went on singing. Not the slightest vibration in his voice could have hinted that something might be happening. The buzzing became louder and louder. Unperturbed, Peter went on singing. And then came the BANG! Near enough but not for us. We could relax. Peter finished his song. The audience remained motionless – bemused. One did not yet clap in churches in those days in Britain. Peter bowed. The concert went on. It had just been one of those days.

Paris had only just been liberated. But France was still under the dark spell of war. I wanted my compatriots – who had been shut off from the outside world for four long years – to hear as soon as possible the best that Britain had to offer in the way of music. With the help of Madame de Fels, President of France–Grande Bretagne, I had managed to organize a recital for Ben and Peter at the Salle Gaveau. But there was a problem. Even in the best hotels hot water was scarce. Where were they to change, etc.? At last I found a friend in whose flat they could enjoy that supreme luxury: a sizzling hot bath. The concert was a triumph. But the house only half full. Who indeed in France had then heard about this young composer, that tenor, from 'the land without music', as the French still considered Britain – and still would for quite some time?

Peter was of course a marvellous exponent and great lover of French music. 'Nobody – except perhaps Bernac – sings "Tel jour, telle nuit" like Peter,' Poulenc used to say.

Time had marched on. The war belonged to old-time memories and history books. A new world had emerged from the old. And a disease – festivalitis – spread its rash from one country to another. In southern France a slogan was born: *Provence, Terre des Festivals* – Provence, Land of Festivals. Every summer indeed hundreds of events – at present, they are said to have reached the astronomical total of a thousand – spring up in city after city, village after village. But, musically at least, the most important one has always been – and still is – Aix-en-Provence. And it is there that, in 1951, Ben and Peter, still very little known in France, but already surrounded by an aura of fame for the cognoscenti, were asked to give a recital in the courtyard of the Aix city hall. Tapestries hung from the ancient walls. There were flowers everywhere. And Peter and Ben performed one of those programmes in which they always have been unique. Song after song filled the air with poetic sound. (Even after all these years I cannot enter the Cour de l'Hôtel de Ville without hearing Peter's soft voice, his impeccable phrasing, conjuring up the distant past.) The audience was bewitched. Encores were asked for – and generously given. I knew that Ben had brought with him that collection of French folk songs that he had so splendidly arranged. Yet the concert ended and none had been performed. 'Why didn't you do any of the French songs?' asked I after the performance was over. 'Oh no!' said Ben with a wry smile. 'Not in France!' 'You see?' whispered Peter. 'That's how he is.'

Yehudi Menuhin

PETER PEARS

I would say that, from the joyous experience of those seasons at Aldeburgh I shared with Ben and Peter, the foremost quality that emerged in our growing knowledge of him was his extraordinary and unique balance.

Ben was quicksilver, all nerve and movement. Peter was deep calm illuminated by delicious humour. He reminded one of one's ideal of a bishop, witty, warm, reliable, wise, totally incapable of petty reaction while totally capable of cold fury in the face of any act he deemed as moral turpitude. One sunny day we actually enjoyed a free afternoon – no rehearsal, no performance, simply Suffolk, the sea air, the balm that is the English seaside. Peter suggested a game of croquet. I, not being brought up in that especial English delight befitting a free summer afternoon, agreed so long as both would accept a tyro in their midst.

Diana, of course, had played since early childhood and only her career and my marriage had divorced her from her passion for that lovely game.

Ben and Diana formed one partnership and poor dear Peter had to accept me as someone who having only learnt to wield a violin and bow was ill equipped to tackle a mallet and those strange multicoloured balls I was told I had to manoeuvre through white metal hoops, disposed at strict distances I might add, upon the somewhat bumpy lawn of the Red House.

I showed all the desperate desire of the devotedly unskilled to live up to my partner's worthiness. Peter illustrated in that silly and unimportant game all those qualities of sweetness, gentleness, co-operation and harmony of mind and heart that have made him one of the greatest and subtlest of musicians it has been my good fortune to have worked with. As I bashed and slashed at the obstinate ball, missing hoops, posts and shamefacedly retrieving it from a clump of lupins, Peter smiled with gentle encouragement, and with that impeccable rhythm, which is another of his wonderful musical gifts, managed to retrieve our partnership from total disaster. Ben and Diana of course won – but Peter made me feel that winning was utterly unimportant – companionship was all.

Sieglinde Mesirca

ORPHEUS

wenn er seine Stimme
aufhob und sang
hielt die Welt
den Atem an
und lauschte –
an der hohen Grenze
hinüber
hoben Engel
wachsam ihre Flügel
denn auch die Lüfte
des Himmels
waren bewegt
und Götter lächelten
sich zu.

Dearest Peter,

'I wonder as I wander' – als ich dieses Lied 1956 in Düsseldorf zum ersten Mal von Dir hörte, hatte auch ich 'die Stimme von Orpheus' wahrhaft vernommen. Dieser unvergessliche Eindruck vertiefte sich durch alle Deine Konzerte, die ich von da an, wo immer es möglich war, besuchte.

Wenn ich an Dich und Dein Singen denke, sind Ben und seine Musik immer mit eingeschlossen, eine zweisame All-Einheit.

Ich müsste komponieren, singen und sagen können wie Benjamin Britten und Peter Pears, um all das zum Ausdruck zu bringen was uns verbindet, was ich mit und durch sie erlebt habe und was sich nun, wie ein Kaleidoskop aus Edelsteinen und Sternstunden, vor meinem inneren Auge, meinem inneren Hören dreht: 'I wonder as I wander'.

Ihr habt eine herrliche Brücke menschlich-musikalischer Beziehungen zwischen Aldeburgh (England) und Elmau (Deutschland) mit bauen helfen; wieviele Menschen sind auf dieser Brücke immer wieder zu neuen Ufern des Verstehens und der Freundschaft hin- und hergewandert.

Durch die vielen, von Euch aufgeführten musikalischen Werke von Old-England bis in unsere Zeit, von Henry Purcell bis Benjamin Britten, dem 'Purcell unserer Zeit', sind Türen und Tore zwischen Menschen und Ländern aufgegangen, viele Menschen konnten durch Euch neu hören und verstehen lernen.

In mir ist ein Bild entstanden: Du und Ben als 'Säulenheilige' vor einem Tempel, zwischen denen unzählige Menschen in das Tempelinnere strömen, um durch Musik, die unmissverständlichste Sprache, zu erfahren, was es heisst, wirklich Mensch zu sein.

1959 haben wir in Elmau unter Leitung von Hans Oppenheim mit Dir, Benjamin Britten, Julian Bream und mit den Saltire Singers die Britisch–Deutschen Musiktage zum erstenmal durchgeführt. In diesem Jahr fanden sie zum 27. Mal statt. Wie dankbar sind wir Dir, Peter, dass auch Du wieder dabei warst und die Tradition, dieser in der Welt einzigartigen Britisch–Deutschen Musiktage aufrecht erhältst. Sie werden vielleicht von Deinem ehemaligen Schüler Neil Mackie und seinen Freunden weiterhin fortgesetzt?

Diese Musiktage haben mit dazu beigetragen, dass berühmte und junge Künstler immer wieder anfragen, ob sie in Elmau, dem 'bayerischen Kultur-zentrum', auch einmal auftreten dürfen? Ihr Künstler alle tragt dazu bei, die Aufgabe der Elmau als Begegnungsstätte im Sinn von Johannes Müller lebendig zu erhalten, d. h. den Menschen nicht nur zu einer äusseren, sondern vor allem zu einer *inneren Erholung* und Besinnung zu verhelfen. Hier in Elmau können sie auch erleben, was es heisst, ein Mensch zu sein.

Viele glückliche Stunden menschlich-musikalischer Freundschaft hatten wir miteinander seit 1959. Heitere und ernste Erlebnisse haben uns ergriffen und begeistert. Von den Herz und Sinn bewegenden Konzerten über 'Britten-Torte', bis zum fliegenden Tanzschritt auf Langlaufskieren oder gemütlichem Zusammensitzen bei Kerzenlicht und gutem Wein.

Als wir mit Ben einmal über die sich ständig wiederholenden Missverständnisse zwischen Menschen und Umwelt sprachen meinte ich: 'Die Hauptsache ist, dass man wirklich lieben kann, dann hört das Missverstehen auf.' Ben antwortete: 'You said real love is the main thing? I tell you: it is the only thing.'

In diesem Sinn, dearest Peter, umgibt Dich eine Schutzmauer aus guten Gedanken von allen Menschen in der Welt, die Dich singend und sprechend erlebt haben und kennenlernen durften.

Eine Schutzmauer aus Liebe, Freundschaft, Verehrung, Bewunderung und unendlicher Dankbarkeit.

Yours ever,

BOBBI

['I wonder as I wander' – when I heard this song sung by you on the first day of May 1956 in Düsseldorf, I knew that I had truly discovered 'the voice of Orpheus'. This unforgettable experience deepened at all your concerts, which from then on I attended whenever I could.

I have only to think of you and your singing for Ben and his music to be there as well, a two-sided but completely single experience.

If only I could compose, sing and tell with the expressive power of Benjamin Britten and Peter Pears of what joins us, of what I've experienced with and through them, and of what now turns before my mind's eye and ear like a kaleidoscope of jewels and starry hours: 'I wonder as I wander'.

You have helped to build a wonderful bridge of human and musical connections between Aldeburgh in England and Elmau in Germany; so many people have crossed this bridge travelling to and fro to new shores of understanding and friendship.

Through your many performances of musical works from 'Old England' up to today, from Henry Purcell to Benjamin Britten, the 'Purcell of our age', doors and gates have been opened between people and countries, and many people have learned anew to listen and to understand.

I have a picture in my mind of you and Ben as 'sacred pillars' before a temple: between them countless people stream in to experience, through music – the language least given to misunderstanding – what it means to be truly human.

In 1959 the Anglo-German Music Days in Elmau took place for the first time under the direction of Hans Oppenheim, yourself, Benjamin Britten and Julian Bream, and with the Saltire Singers taking part. This year sees their twenty-seventh anniversary. We are grateful to you, Peter, for again being there to keep alive this unique Anglo-German musical event. Perhaps the tradition will be continued by your former pupil Neil Mackie and his friends?

These Music Days have caused famous as well as young artists to ask repeatedly whether they may perform at Elmau, the 'Bavarian Cultural Centre'. All you artists help to keep alive the task of Elmau as a meeting place in Johannes Müller's sense: of affording inner as well as outer rest and recuperation for the spirit. Here in Elmau they can experience what it means to be a human being.

Since 1959 we have shared many happy hours of musical friendship, of carefree as well as serious experiences. They range from heart-stirring concerts, via 'Britten-Torte' to gliding dance steps on cross-country skis, or just sitting cosily together with good wine by candlelight.

I remember that when we were once talking with Ben about the persistent misunderstandings between man and his environment I said: 'The main thing is to be able to love, and then all misunderstandings will cease.' Ben replied: 'You said real love is the main thing? I tell you: it is the only thing.'

In this sense, dearest Peter, you are surrounded by a protective wall of the warm thoughts of everyone who has come to know you through your singing and through personal contact with you. A protective wall of love, friendship, respect, admiration and boundless gratitude.]

Donald Mitchell

MYTHIC PEARS: IDOMENEO AND OEDIPUS

So many memories of so many performances, of Ben's works, of course, but also of works by many other composers, of our own time, as Ben was, and by his great predecessors. First a recollection of Mozart's *Idomeneo* at Aldeburgh in 1969, an English Opera Group production that Ben conducted. A fateful year that – the year of the fire – but the conflagration brought us one inestimable bonus, in the shape of *Idomeneo* repeated in the rebuilt Maltings in the 1970 Festival.

The 1969 performance had defeated the ruins and ashes of the Maltings Mark 1 by miraculously transporting itself to a makeshift stage at Blythburgh, with borrowed costumes and improvised lighting. But there was absolutely nothing makeshift about the performance. Indeed, it was in those extraordinary and hectic circumstances that I heard you give what I shall always remember as one of your very finest dramatic interpretations, in the opera's title role.

How can one sum up the impression of that evening in a few words? One can't; but I'll have a shot at it all the same. Nobility; passion; and *radiance*: three words only, but they serve as indicators, at least, of the principal characteristics of your performance. But then one might argue that these qualities are veritable hallmarks of your art as a singer, not only in Mozart (and by the way, a salute to the most civilized of Taminos!) but in most of your other roles as well. (Quint? Not precisely noble, I concede, but certainly a dangerous radiance in his own right.)

I remember too Ben's quite remarkable conducting of *Idomeneo*, and above all his marvellous conception of the tiny instrumental March in F (Act II), which glowed with an interior light – the combination of a perfectly judged slow tempo, hushed dynamics, exquisite phrasing and Cecil Aronowitz's rapt viola playing – which I have never heard matched elsewhere. (I was speaking to a member of the English Chamber Orchestra only the other day about the performance and it was the March that he too recalled as a sublime moment, so intense and transfiguring was *its* radiance.)

Nobility; passion; radiance: all of them precise adjectives (not tired superlatives) which serve equally well to describe your participation in a masterpiece of the twentieth century, with the composer conducting – not a work of Britten's, however, but by Stravinsky. In 1951 you made a gramophone recording of *Oedipus Rex*. What a performance! The most arresting interpretation of Oedipus known to me. (Perhaps there's something about Greek mythology that brings out the best in you.) It is an interpretation that offers *nobility*; there could be nothing more regal than the energy and brilliant rhythm you bring to Oedipus' opening baroque rhetoric – 'Liberi, vos liberabo'; *passion*, by means of which you carve a sentient Oedipus out of Stravinsky's sculpted characterization of his hero, without one whit diminishing Oedipus' mythic status – on the contrary you realize the feeling that the composer himself has embodied (embedded) in 'Invidia fortunam odit', perhaps the most beautiful of all his baroque-inspired arias (there is a counterpart in the Violin Concerto); and finally, *radiance*, the tragic light that dawns along with Oedipus' self-realization of the truth: 'Lux facta est!', his final words and the last of his music, *dis*-passionately sung, as befits a king and an interpretation which unerringly distinguishes between feeling and sentiment.

Your final achievement, it seems to me – and I am certain this is an *Oedipus Rex* that will live on as exemplar and source of illumination – is something quite extraordinary, though it won't come as a surprise to your admirers: how you make a so-called 'dead' language come wholly to life. I am thinking of such things as your duet with percussion, 'Ego senem kekidi', or 'Thebas eruam' (with those ringing, confident repeated notes from which the doomed Oedipus all too soon is to be dislodged) or that stunning bit of declamation 'Stipendarius es, Tiresia!'. In short, you show just the same mastery in Latin, and reveal just the same vocal techniques, whereby words colour the music and music articulates the words, as in any other of the languages you have at your command. Nobility; passion; radiance. But I find myself compelled to add: sensibility; and supreme *intelligence*.

Henry Moore

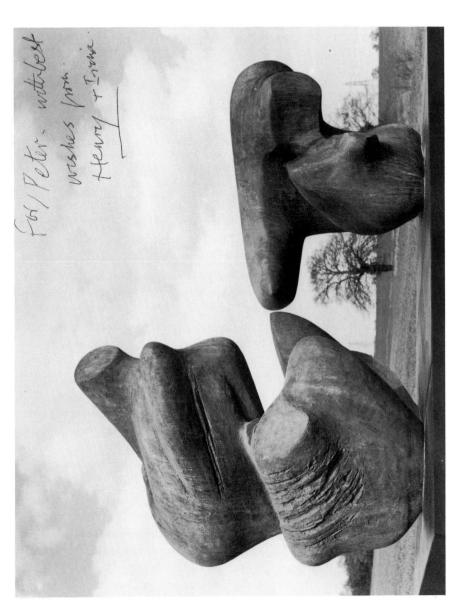

Two Piece Reclining Figure: Points (1969) (bronze; length, c. 12 ft)

Murray Perahia

It is a very special pleasure to celebrate Peter Pears's 75th birthday and to wish him much happiness and many happy returns. Personally, it is also a time to be grateful, as he has always been a very important part of my life, both as a musician and as a colleague and friend. And in both cases what makes Peter unique is his transcending ability to be so completely himself, and to be natural and spontaneous. Peter asserts his individuality without force, in fact with grace and ease. Musically, his voice and its inflection and phrasing immediately come to mind. Few dare to sing so personally or so truly. Once one has heard it, one will never forget it. It is so unusual. It has a haunting quality and a darkness. The first time I heard it was on a recording of the *Winterreise*. Hearing him and Ben re-create Schubert's immortal vision of despair with all the warmth and searing pain the music contains, was a revelation to me. The impact was so strong that I was determined to go to every concert they did in New York, four in all. Those were amazing hours of music-making: the composer re-creating his and others' music, reorchestrating, reshaping, re-living; the singer reacting to all of this mostly by searching his emotions and making them fresh and vibrant so that a real dialogue existed – maybe this was similar to Vogl and Schubert.

I remember vividly how almost an entire audience was crying and embracing each other after a *Dichterliebe* performance, or chuckling delightedly through 'The Plough Boy' and 'The foggy, foggy dew'. Years later, when I had the privilege of working with Peter, we covered a wide repertoire, going through many of Ben's cycles. The power and intensity of Peter's expression was as fresh as ever. By the genuineness of his emotional response to all the music we did he gave me a glimpse of his very special musical world, a contemporary-real world unsullied by clichés, routines, accepted traditions, etc.

In personal relationships, the same respect for individuality, whether his own or the other person's, held. Respectful and interested, one can speak freely with Peter and get a frank response. In collaborating on the Festival plans, his individuality gives his ideas a kind of poetry because they always originate in his enthusiasms. Practicality is not a priority, but dreaming and daring are.

In a time when mechanization, routine and alienation are the norm, Peter's voice, both figuratively and literally, speaks a different language. In clear ringing sounds, it touches one, it moves one, it involves our emotions – it has frailty and strength. It is a testament to what is unique in all of us – the free human spirit. It is a rare gift that can express that. Peter – many thanks for all you have meant to us and for all you have given us.

Sue Phipps

Dearest Peter,

On this great day we Phippses wish you the happiest of all your birthdays.

To my delight – and I hope yours too – I found that according to your Chinese horoscope you were born in the year of the DOG.

> The martial strains have summoned me
> To hear your sorrows,
> Still your pain.
> I am the protector of Justice;
> Equality – my sole friend.
> My vision never blurred by cowardice,
> My soul never chained,
> Life without honour
> Is life in vain.
>
> I AM THE DOG.

This may be the most lovable sign of all the Chinese cycle. A person born in the year of the Dog is honest, intelligent and straightforward. He has a deep sense of loyalty and a passion for justice and fair play. Like the late Zhou Enlai, who was born in the year of the Dog, the native of this sign will be loved for his warm charisma and superb insight into human nature. With his astute intelligence and noble character, he makes a good but somewhat reluctant leader. People trust him and hold him in high esteem because of his sense of duty and discretion. Most people born under this sign are tough, in the sense that they can take a lot of stress without cracking up. The Dog's stable mind makes him a good counsellor, priest or psychologist. During times of crisis he can suffer hardship and deprivation without complaining. He earnestly wishes that the world were a better place to live in and he will not be afraid to go out and do something about it. Many saints and martyrs were born under the idealistic sign of the Dog.

The metal element combined with this lunar sign, which is also governed by metal, produces a double metal sign which is extremely formidable. Tibetans call this combination the 'Iron Dog', and look upon its year with much apprehension. The iron dog will exercise strong mental discipline over himself and take things very seriously.

The acute sensitivity of the Crab is intertwined here with the internal balance of the Dog. This sign will revere beauty and purity. The Cancerian Dog will display a natural affection for others and establish noble standards for himself, while living a refined but moderate life-style.

So this is where your towering strength, warmth and integrity come from – the loving and loyal DOG! GOD be with you on your 75th birthday and for always,

love,

SUE

John Piper

Santa Maria dei Miracoli, Venice (1964) (lithograph; 38 × 39.2cms)

Myfanwy Piper

Dear Peter,

It is lovely to take part in a celebration for you who have offered so many and such marvellous celebrations to your friends. Quite apart from the sound of your voice, which Ben has celebrated for all of us for ever, you are a born celebrator. That is not only to say that you are good at elegant soirées, or at backstage parties, picnics, routs or taking the cork out of a bottle at the exact, gasping moment, but that you have an impulse to turn what may already be an enjoyable and rewarding occasion into an unforgettable one. I think of the time when you and Ben stayed at Fawley Bottom on your way to give a concert in Oxford; you were not looking forward to it much. In the evening we worked on something that we were all involved in, *Owen Wingrave* it may have been, then, more relaxed, and concerts forgotten, we talked of Don Ottavio, and what an inspired wet he was – you were working on him at the time. 'Shall we give them a song?' you said and did, with Ben at the piano. It was a stunning performance of 'Dalla sua pace' *and* 'Il mio tesoro' for an audience of two. All your friends have experienced that kind of generosity at some time or another.

I remember too how a whole audience laughed with delight and shared in the welcome when you introduced Lutoslawski at a concert in London. No formal introduction, but a cascade of wit, affection and enthusiasm.

As well as these reminiscences, which could go on for ever, especially if I were to begin to describe journeys – but they are your brilliant prerogative – I want to talk about words. When I began work on *The Turn of the Screw* I was an inexperienced and terrified librettist – indeed, not a librettist at all, and you gave me enormous help, both consciously and unconsciously and continued to do so with the other two librettos. I didn't hear the first *Peter Grimes*, alas, but after that, as you know, because of John's involvement I was able to go to rehearsals and performances of every opera that Ben wrote. My ears and my mind became filled with his music and with his way with language. When I first explored the story and wrote tentative bits of dialogue for *The Screw* I was accompanied by a ghost of sound, no, not even sound, but a sensuous apprehension of how it would be clothed, and given life in Ben's hands. But when it came to tackling big lyrical pieces – Quint's song and later the Wingrave ballad, Aschenbach's praise of Venice, the appallingly difficult paraphrase from Plato – then it was the sound of your voice that came naturally to my ears. Through it and my memories of your performances I was able to find a way to commit myself to lines which I should never have had the courage to do if they had been written to be spoken. It was your love of words, your response to all possible meanings, your lucid, generous phrasing that inspired me. It was your clear-sightedness too, as well as Ben's, that detected pretensions, false or tactless words and unnecessary embellishments. Thank you for it all.

It is impossible to think of either you or Ben without the other. Your life together was and still is a double celebration. I salute you both with love and admiration.

MYFANWY

Mary Potter: *Reeds* (oils)

Priaulx Rainier

'Chant' (5) and 'Fire' (6) from *The Bee Oracles* (1969). Words by Edith Sitwell. Autograph manuscript

Stephen Reiss

In the 1950s this country contracted what came to be known as festival fever. Festivals were springing up everywhere and no self-respecting town or village felt content without one. By now the rash has somewhat subsided, and the latest fad is the arts centre, or the 'centre of excellence' according to the official parlance. Whether this is progress remains to be seen, and is a matter that can be debated at some other time.

The model festival, the archetype, the most imitated, was Aldeburgh. It had two priceless possessions, Ben and Peter. They gave much more than their personal performances, important though these were; they concerned themselves with every detail, exhibitions, lectures, bus tours, the programme book. They sat on every committee and nothing escaped their notice. In their hands the Festival became much more than the sum of its parts, it truly became a work of art.

In this case Peter was the principal composer, the first sketches were invariably his. Except as regards those events in which he personally was involved, Ben adopted the position of critic and arbiter.

Composition would begin just as the previous Festival was ending. Some of the performers would be invited to return, others were simply thanked. Fortunately those who would normally have their diaries full years in advance had kept the dates free, just in case. On the brief 'holiday' that immediately followed the Festival the entire plan was formed. In this way each Festival was seen afresh and the most recent lessons were learned.

We salute Peter for many things: great singer, great actor, teacher, diplomat, and great composer of festivals, with thirty-eight already to his credit. Has there ever been, or will there ever be, a greater? I do not believe it possible.

Ceri Richards

Mstislav Rostropovich and Galina Vishnevskaya

Дорогой Питерчик!

К твоему 75-летию мы возносим тебе благодарность двух, связанных жизнью и музыкой сердец, за то счастье, которое ты нам дал.

Это счастье как-бы двойное: счастье твоей дружбы и счастье общения с твоим неповторимым искусством.

Любая музыкальная встреча с тобой на протяжении последних 25ти лет - на репетициях или на концертах - для нас не только радость сопричастия к твоему творчеству, но и всегда школа, в которой мы многому учимся, не переставая восхищаться гармонией твоего многообразного таланта, соеденившей в неповторимое целое твой магический голос, которым ты выражаешь тончайшие и сложнейшие движения души, энциклопедическую музыкальную эрудицию, талант актёра и педагога.

Галлерея оперных образов, созданных тобой, заполнившая всё оперное пространство гениального Бена, от «Питера Граймса» до «Смерти в Венеции», заполнила и наши жизни. Никогда не могут потускнеть переживания, полученные нами от «Поворота винта» в Эдинбурге, «Альберта Херинга» в Ленинграде, Церковных опер в Орфорде и Лондоне, «Смерть в Венеции» в Молтинг Снейпе.

Масштабы и контрасты красок в твоей палитре и в репертуаре просто поразительны: от неповторимого в своей юношеской страсти Ромео (в дуэте с Галей), до наивного и очаровательного мальчика-Пети из «Пети и волка» Прокофьева (со Славой, как дирижёром).

И ко всему этому твои Шуберт, Бах и старинные фольклорные песни - и всё в твоем исполнении такое естественное, всё - в своей первозданной красоте! Мы никогда не забудем, как Галина, перед её первым исполнением «Миссы Солемнис» Бетховена, спросила тебя о темпах, а ты сел за рояль и свободно сыграл по партитуре всё произведение.

И может быть во всём огромном твоём творчестве есть два такта, которые в нашей памяти сохраняются, как драгоценный бриллиант - это конед Агнус Дэй из Военного реквиема Бриттена, когда в этой последней фразе ты буквально возносишь нас в небеса, к твоему последнему фа диезу! Боже, как нам трудно было после этого - одного из нас заставить дальше продолжать дирижировать, а другую заставить дальше петь!!

Дорогой наш, любимый Петенька!

Твоя щедрая дружба к нам сделала нашу жизнь много богаче: знать тебя не только как великого артиста, но и как близкого друга – всегда исключительная привилегия для нас. В совместных путешествиях по Великобритании и России, в долгих застольных вечеров, в гостях у Пушкина в Михайловском и у Шостаковича в Жуковке мы счастливы были познать и оценить тебя, как нашего любимого и доброго друга.

Мы счастливы попасть в книгу поздравлений тебе, в книгу твоих друзей, которая будет достаточно толстой, но могла бы быть и такой, как «Энциклопедия Британника».

И всё же, всё лучшее, что есть в этой книге, можно выразить только двумя словами: ПИТЕР ПИРЗ!

По старой русской традиции, мы в год тоего 75-летия поём тебе «многая лета», зная, что наши два голоса растворятся в многомиллионном хоре твоих поклонников.

Всегда твои

Галя Вишневская и Слава Ростропович

Medieval scribes sometimes took the opportunity to sneak in a phrase or two of their own at the end of some completed manuscript. As the transcriber of the Vishnevskaya–Rostropovich contribution, let me add my own voice, and Christina's, to the great birthday chorus of your friends and join the Slavonic section of the choir with that heartfelt *mnogie leta* initiated by Galina and Mstislav.

With gratitude for all your marvellous work and with warm good wishes for this festive day,

SERGEI HACKEL

[On your 75th birthday we offer you the gratitude of two hearts, united in music and in life, for the happiness that you have given us – a kind of double happiness arising, first from your friendship and then from your unique art.

Every musical encounter with you in the last twenty-five years, whether at rehearsal or in the concert hall, has meant not only the joy of sharing in your work as an artist – it has also been a school in which we have learned much, while never ceasing to be delighted by the harmony existing between your many artistic gifts – that unique combination of a magical voice, capable of expressing the most delicate and complex nuances of feeling, an encyclopaedic musical knowledge and extraordinary gifts as both actor and teacher.

The gallery of operatic roles that you have created covers the whole operatic output of the brilliant Ben from *Peter Grimes* to *Death in Venice*. We shall never forget the experience of hearing you in *The Turn of the Screw* at Edinburgh, in

Albert Herring in Leningrad, in the church operas at Orford and in London, and in *Death in Venice* at the Maltings.

The sheer skill and mastery of colour contrasts in both your singing and your repertory are simply staggering! From the unique youthful passion of your Romeo (with Galya) to the delightful naivety of your boyish Petya in Prokofiev's *Peter and the Wolf* (with Slava conducting). And on top of all this your Schubert, your Bach, your folk songs, in which everything has a naturalness and a kind of primordial freshness. Nor shall we ever forget the time when Galya asked your advice about tempi before singing her first *Missa Solemnis*, and you just sat at the piano playing the whole work from the score.

Perhaps of all the things in your huge repertory what stands out in our memories like a rare diamond is the end of the *Agnus Dei* in the *War Requiem* – that last phrase, in which you transported us to heaven with your final F sharp!

God knows how hard we both found it after that to make ourselves go back, one of us to his conducting, the other to her singing.

Dear friend Petenka! your generous friendship has enriched our lives – knowing you not only as a great artist but as a close friend has always been a privilege. Those journeys together in Great Britain and Russia, those long evenings dining together, whether with Pushkin at Mikhailovskoe or with Shostakovich at Tukovka – how happy we were to get to know you and appreciate you as a dear and valued friend!

And now we are happy to find a place in this book of congratulations, a book of your friends, one that will no doubt be fairly thick but could be as thick as the *Encyclopaedia Britannica*.

And yet all that is best in the book can be expressed in just two words – PETER PEARS!

In accordance with old Russian custom we raise our voices on this 75th birthday of yours and wish you 'mnogie leta!' – many years more, knowing that our voices are only two in the chorus of your myriad admirers.

Always yours,

GALYA and SLAVA]

Paul Sacher

Dearest Peter,

What a wonderful time we had together with Ben! Since 1948 we have met time and time again to perform countless works by Purcell, Handel, Mozart, Stravinsky, Walton, Binet, Ringger and, more than anyone, Benjamin Britten. Our concerts have taken place in London and in different Swiss cities, mainly with my Basle Chamber Orchestra and with the Collegium Musicum Zürich.

Ben's music has accompanied us through the decades. A special event was the world première of his *Cantata Academica* on the occasion of the 500th anniversary of Basle University.

I will never forget our first *Serenade* with Dennis Brain, nor our last concert together with the Collegium Musicum Zürich on 28 May 1980, where you gave Rolf Urs Ringger's *Shelley-Songs* their first performance, and where, in Ben's *Illuminations*, you celebrated a great personal triumph. I always hear in my mind the parts that Ben wrote for you, in your interpretation and in your voice.

Please accept, dear Peter, this expression of my gratitude for the joy that our music-making has given me, and my eternal friendship.

PAUL SACHER

The Aldeburgh Festival pays its respects to Edward Fitzgerald: *Old Fitz and His Music*, Jubilee Hall, Aldeburgh, 26 June 1977. *Left to right:* Norman Scarfe, Peter Pears, April Cantelo, Rosamund Strode and Steuart Bedford

Norman Scarfe

My dear Peter,

This year, several of us are posting you our birthday love early, to catch the printer: it isn't difficult, for the affection and the admiration are there all the time. We're in fact scribbling these birthday greetings to you at All Saints tide, as you and I and Mary Verney and young Julian Baker are preparing the repeat performance at Bury of the fun we had during the Festival in the library at Ickworth – re-creating the La Rochefoucauld boys' year in Bury in 1784. The Georgian Group applied too late for tickets in June, and asked me if the piece could be repeated. When you heard this, you and Mary and Julian instantly volunteered. You can't imagine how hugely pleased and flattered I felt. Your prodigal generosity with your great gifts is deeply moving, and I must be one of dozens of people who go on being (very agreeably) overwhelmed by it.

This November we approach Ben's 71st birthday. When he lived, Aldeburgh Church seemed like heaven so often through his playing and conducting. But none of us in Aldeburgh Church for his 70th birthday will forget that celebration: Norwich choristers, Ben's *Missa Brevis*, his *Ceremony of Carols* written on that Danish cargo boat as it brought you both (thank Nicolas!) safely back to us across the awful Atlantic in 1942, and Osian irresistibly introducing and performing the Harp Suite: ABOVE ALL, as everyone of us felt, you, bravely and superbly intoning Wystan Auden's 'Song for St Cecilia's Day'.

There you stood. I wondered how much, perhaps unconsciously, people are shaped by their Christian names. The first great role you created was Peter (Grimes) the fisherman. You *are* the rock on which the Festival stands. You've long held keys to heavenly music kingdoms. The wide-aisled church was made centuries ago for such deeply felt occasions. The parson-poet-begetter of Grimes lurked dourly round the corner in marble, facing John Piper's window, glimmering invisibly that evening in artificial light. In daylight its triptych succinctly says you as well as Ben: Prodigal Son forgiven, mother's distracted search for dead son assuaged (what *anguish* you made us share with her in Orford), and the three young men daring that fiery furnace (one can never eat grapes now without remembering your nasty Nebuchadnezzar: in the window, Meshach's expression has an affecting look of Ben).

Chancel arch, puritan pulpit, that church-setting now known the world over, all dissolved as you spoke the ode for Ben's and St Cecilia's Day:

In a garden shady this holy lady
With reverent cadence and subtle psalm.
Like a black swan as death came on
Poured forth her song in perfect calm . . .

Your own birthday's shared with saints Acacius, Albanus, and Paulinus of
Nola, none, I think, notably musical: but at Aldeburgh you share it with all of us
at the Festival. How we look forward to it.

Huge hugs for Rita, from Paul and me, and myriad congratulations from us
both,

NORMAN

Elisabeth Legge-Schwarzkopf

I am convinced that my own opinion about Sir Peter cannot say anything more
enlightening than the 'musical' public knows anyway. That a very English
Englishman could become one of the major German *Lieder*-singers is a miracle
in itself and that goes also for Peter Pears singing the Bach *Evangelisten* in the
Passions.

I am not of course the person to judge or to give a very valid opinion as to him
singing Britten: the other night I was listening via Radio France to a most
incredible and haunting performance of the *Serenade* for tenor, horn and
strings, Britten conducting, Pears singing, the horn was, I believe, Barry
Tuckwell. It was something one cannot wait to hear again and again.

There is no doubt a very special place in the hearts of us foreigners for the like
of those great British artists.

Wishing Sir Peter an equally fruitful life as a teacher – I know he is already
making the greatest impact on young singers –

a colleague,

ELISABETH

William Servaes

Leaving aside, if it is possible, Peter's stature as an artist and thinking about working with and around him for nearly ten years, I remember in particular three qualities with gratitude and admiration. First there is the extraordinary unflappability in numberless moments of last-minute crises to which festivals such as Aldeburgh's are inevitably prone. Then there is the resourcefulness amounting sometimes, I suspect, to enjoyment, in solving the practical problems that stemmed from these. 'After all,' he would say, 'if the worst comes to the worst *I* can always do something' and that is often exactly what he and Ben did. Finally there is the courage; courage after Ben's death to keep the flag flying, and courage to face up to and minimize the effects of his recent afflictions – courage, in fact, whatever the circumstances, to go on being uncompromisingly and indestructibly PETER PEARS.

Dear Peter, Pat and I salute you and send you our love,

BILL

Peter Stansky and William Abrahams

DOUBLE IMAGE

We have three memories of Peter Pears that we would like to record on the occasion of his 75th birthday, one historical and two personal. Of course we knew his voice well before we ever met him, through hearing him on records. He then became important to us in a more personal and direct way before we met him when we began to look into the making of *Peter Grimes* with particular reference to its relationship to the Second World War. We were taken with the irony that not only was our own country – the United States – of particular importance to the making of the opera, but particularly significant was where we now happen to live, the state of California. Benjamin Britten and Peter Pears were in Escondido in the south of the state in the summer of 1941. Peter Pears discovered in a San Diego bookstore a copy of the collected poems of George Crabbe. And so it started, to climax on 7 June 1945 with the world première of *Peter Grimes*.

Years later, in October 1983, through the kindness of Donald and Kathleen Mitchell, we finally met, to talk of *Peter Grimes* in the Red House in Aldeburgh. We asked about the composition of the opera and Sir Peter told us about a particular phrase in the opera that was changed and changed again in order to get it right, and then he sang the phrase for us. A magical moment.

And then next summer, in June 1984, we came to the Aldeburgh Festival, and had the great pleasure of attending his birthday concert that year, at which Sir Peter read words by Siegfried Sassoon, Walter Pater, Virginia Woolf and Rainer Maria Rilke to music by Robin Holloway. Also there was the first performance of a magnificent *Elegy* for viola, composed by Britten in 1930. And then a lovely birthday party. We remained in Aldeburgh for some days after the Festival working in the Library, greatly assisted by the Librarian, Paul Wilson. The last day we were there, in the afternoon, we watched a video tape of a performance of *Peter Grimes* with Peter Pears. About a half-hour before its conclusion, when the opera is at its most magnificent, we were conscious of a door opening and a presence entering: Pears and Grimes. We knew who was there and at the same time were totally absorbed by what was on the screen. We watched to the end, as the Borough reasserted itself, life went on, oblivious of tragedy. To see Peter Pears in the opera was powerful and wonderful enough, but to see it as he himself stood there at the back of the room gave the occasion a drama and depth that we will never forget and for which we are profoundly grateful.

Mary Potter: *Imogen Holst* (oils; 71 × 56 cms)
This portrait was painted in the spring of 1954 while Imogen was memorizing Bach's *St. John Passion*, which she was to conduct at the Aldeburgh Festival that June. Mary Potter caught the characteristic look of concentration so well known to Imogen's friends.

Rosamund Strode

A vignette from July 1955: the rococo theatre at Schloss Schwetzingen, near Heidelberg, out of season. Peter, demonstrating to his three fascinated car passengers (on the way home from the Ansbach Bach Festival) – and to the resident caretaker – Quint's eerie, honeyed, offstage calls of 'Miles' in this beautiful little theatre, built in 1752 for the Elector Palatine of Mannheim, where the German première of *The Turn of the Screw* had been staged by the English Opera Group only that May. This memory sets up a long train of thought.

Ben, Peter, Imo – the Aldeburgh triple powerhouse. Some of the effects of the influence each one had on the other two, especially during those closely collaborative years of the 1950s, can clearly be traced, like ley-lines on the fields, leading at last towards their recognizable transmutation into Ben's music. There always has to be a first meeting, of course (though somehow with these three that is in itself a difficult concept!) and Imogen had first met Peter and Ben in 1943, when they came to give a recital at Dartington Hall. They returned there more than once, and after a visit in the late summer of 1945 Imo gave them her most prized possession, an early edition (which she had only recently acquired) of Playford's *Harmonia Sacra*. Of course Ben and Peter knew their Purcell already (or thought they did) but this edition, printed so soon after Purcell's death and containing so many of his marvellous and almost unknown set pieces, came like a blaze of light. We can still hear the results in all of Ben's Purcell realizations, from the earliest ones (out of that same *Harmonia Sacra*) to the *Fairy Queen*, in which they all three took a part.

Having Imo resident in Aldeburgh, working as Ben's amanuensis from 1952, fired off Peter with one of his good ideas. She mustn't waste her proven gifts for choir-training, so what about getting together a small group of students and young professionals which she could train, and which might then be used for concert-giving in and out of the Festival? Splendid. (This group met in London on Saturdays, and became the Purcell Singers.) Then there was the amateur chorus for the Festival, which Imogen trained in Ipswich during the winter months. And finally – this must have been rather a relief to Imo, who was entirely dependent upon public transport for all these journeys (though trains still came to Aldeburgh station) – there were the weekly meetings of the Aldeburgh Music Club, those friendly and enthusiastic gatherings of more or less musical neighbours (of all standards of attainment) then held in Crag

House itself. It was, of course, Imo who taught her two distinguished colleagues to play the recorder – Ben the descant and treble, Peter the treble and bass (whose idea was *that*? Or was it the residual hankerings of the schoolboy bassoon player at Lancing, still largely unfulfilled?) – which one can detect in the Fairies' 'tongs and bones' music in *A Midsummer Night's Dream* as well as in the *Scherzo* written for and dedicated to the Club, and unforgettably played by them, with *Alpine Suite*, at the 1955 Festival, the performers seated in punts on Thorpeness Meare. And Imogen used to describe an extraordinary moment of revelation she once witnessed as the Music Club, out carol singing one still, dark night, straggled its way up the Town Steps to the tune of (I think) Tallis's Canon. By the time the leaders had reached the Terrace, the last voices were well behind in time and space, so that the canon itself was anything but true. Ben (somewhere in the middle) stood stock still half-way up the steps, transfixed by the magic of the trailing voices. Isn't this what we all heard much later, in *Curlew River*?

The Purcell Singers became well known to Aldeburgh Festival audiences, but we also gave concerts in London and elsewhere, usually of unaccompanied music. Sometimes we shared a concert with both Peter and Ben, and at other times Peter would come on his own, perhaps singing the Evangelist in one of the Schütz Passions, or the Spirit of the Masque to add authenticity to our performance of the Choral Dances from *Gloriana*, a frequent end-of-programme item. But then the concert would also include unaccompanied songs for solo tenor; new works written for him at Peter's own request, folk songs (such as 'Down in yon forest' and 'I wonder as I wander') – and monodic medieval settings of liturgical texts, to which Imo had introduced him. The one that always seemed to suit him best and which he sang with extraordinary flexibility, passion and concentration was the piece that opened the Purcell Singers' concert given at the 1954 Festival, 'Beata viscera Mariae virginis', written in about 1190 by Pérotin, composer of Notre-Dame, Paris. Peter's beautifully controlled singing of its rapid melismatic phrases suggested to Ben exactly what he wanted for Quint's unearthly and alluring calls to Miles in *The Turn of the Screw*, the work he was writing that summer.

This, then, is where we came in: the three of us (and the caretaker) sitting in the deserted theatre at Schwetzingen thirty years ago, gazing at an empty stage while Quint sang his haunting phrases out of sight.

Marshall B. Sutton

Dear Peter,

Your friends of The Canadian Aldeburgh Foundation – directors, members, supporters and beneficiaries – join me in sending you, our Patron, affectionate birthday greetings. The brevity of our association in no way diminishes the warmth of our wishes or our deep appreciation of the active role you have played personally in our work. We shall never forget the magnificent recital you gave with Osian Ellis in Toronto in November 1976 to launch the Foundation, a most generous gesture and a miraculous evening of Purcell, Schubert, Ravel and Britten.

The Foundation dates from its formal establishment in 1975 but its origins go back to the twenty-third festival in 1970 when Françoise, 12-year-old Philip and I arrived in Aldeburgh for the first time on a June afternoon, after a tiring transatlantic flight. After settling in at the Wentworth, we set out upon the then deserted Crag Path to try and combat the effects of jet lag. It was a reassuring omen that the first person we saw, standing on the shingle near the lifeboat with his dog, was Benjamin Britten gazing out to sea.

The final concert of that festival was entitled *Up She Goes Again . . .* You will recall that members of the Cambridge Ballooning Club were due on that occasion to wind up the festival with an ascent. It was a memorable and high-spirited afternoon, undampened by the failure of the balloon to go up due to the threat of thunderstorms!

To date, The Canadian Aldeburgh Foundation has assisted almost fifty young Canadian singers and instrumentalists to study with you and other outstanding teachers at the Britten–Pears School. Many of them have now taken their place in the Canadian and international world of music. They and we acknowledge with gratitude your personal interest in their careers. The feelings of all are summed up by one young singer in a letter to us written on her return to Canada:

> . . . just being with Peter Pears for three weeks was a rich and rare experience. We lived with his voice, as he sang and as he spoke; with his love and respect for the songs, their poets and their composers; with his grief; with his magnificent gestures that outdo Charlie Chaplin; with his dancing eyes and his most tender smile. Everything he sings is filled with his whole life. That is the biggest lesson I have learned.

On this your 75th birthday, Françoise and I send you our warmest wishes for many happy returns of the day.

Bon anniversaire et meilleurs voeux de nous tous!

Yours sincerely,

MARSHALL

Frank Taplin

Suffolk, salt marshes and the sea, the Sailors' Walk, Saxon Snape and Iken; Orford, Blythburgh, Thorpeness and Lavenham; the Maltings, Jubilee Hall, the Red House – these and many other images rush to the mind of one who loves Aldeburgh.

As an American Friend of the Aldeburgh Festival and past President of the Metropolitan Opera, I have been fortunate in counting Peter Pears as a friend over the years and in having seen at Aldeburgh and elsewhere the depth of his contribution as an artist of rare and discriminating talents.

His performances on the Metropolitan Opera stage of Captain Vere in *Billy Budd* and Aschenbach in *Death in Venice* were unforgettable realizations of these roles. Met artists generally make their débuts on our stage at an earlier age than 64, but, in having done just this as Aschenbach, Peter Pears showed that the years had not diminished that lively and youthful spirit, that innate musicality, with which he has been blessed.

Few individuals maintain a life of artistic excellence over so long a span as Peter Pears has done. Faithful friend and collaborator of Benjamin Britten, he was 'present at the creation' of so many of Britten's important works, adding often his own creative role in shaping their performances. Town and Festival alike breathe the spirit of Britten and Pears, and we joyfully acknowledge their vision and leadership in this artistic enterprise, which has engaged Sir Peter for almost forty years.

We can be grateful too that Sir Peter in his later years has played a leading role as co-founder of the Britten–Pears School of Advanced Musical Studies. It performs an important function in setting standards and in giving young artists the coaching and guidance they require at an early stage in their careers. This aspect of his work, in which the American Friends of the Aldeburgh Festival take a special interest, ensures that his artistic influence will live beyond his own time.

To our friend at 75: thank you, and may your flame burn brightly in the years ahead. We, for our part, will always wish to respond to your siren song from Aldeburgh: 'Come again! Sweet love doth now invite.'

Rita Thomson

Dear Peter,

It's your birthday, you must choose your birthday dinner!! What will it be? Oysters? Steak? Scallops? Perhaps a curry? Your parents, who lived so much of their married life in India, left you the legacy of a penchant for this. Wasn't it your father who said one could curry anything, even an old boot?

Do you remember, Peter, the occasion in Horham when you decided to make one of your famous curries for Ben and me and yourself? Soon it was ready and we attacked it with gusto. As you and I finished off the last few delicious mouthfuls there was a plaintive cry from Ben – 'I don't know about you two but I don't appear to have any meat in my curry.' You had forgotten to add it to the sauce. You and I hadn't even noticed!!

Happy Birthday, dearest Peter, and many many happy returns of today.

Fondest love,

RITA

PS Perhaps we should settle for the last cutting of asparagus with lots of lovely melted butter?

93

Marion Thorpe

Dearest Peter,

My gratitude to you for so many great musical experiences is only tempered by one serious reservation – you have made it almost impossible to listen to your repertoire sung by anyone else! Your singing has revealed to me the magic of works by Schubert, Schumann, Mozart, Bach, Handel, Purcell, Mahler, of folk songs – I can't enumerate them all. You created Ben's works. You have inspired other composers and composers of younger generations to write for you. The deep musical insight and sensitivity of your performances are so indelibly printed on my ear that they have become the absolute and everything else is measured by them.

So you see, you have not only given me profound musical pleasure, but have also made me rather difficult to please! Often, when trying to be charitable after some performance, I think of my father's remark (one of Tony Gishford's favourite ones!) – 'Of course it was bad, but not *so* bad!'

Your generosity in working with young singers at the Britten–Pears School and elsewhere will ensure that your wisdom and experience will be passed on. But your magic will always remain unique to you.

Thank you for 'Dalla sua pace' (alas never on the stage), 'Nacht und Träume', for Flute and Vere and Grimes, for the Evangelist – Oh dear, one should never start naming names, although I don't think you would ever react like the famous violinist, who, when praised for his playing of a particular movement of a work, retorted: 'And what was wrong with the rest of it?'

The privilege of having shared with you and Ben the excitements of planning and achieving so many great musical events is something very precious. It goes right back to St John's Wood High Street days: you and Ben gave shelter to the Steins in 1944, when they had become refugees for the second time after a fire in their Cornwall Gardens flat. I want to include my parents in my birthday wishes to you, remembering the many musical occasions we jointly enjoyed, as well as the fun we all had in the various houses our families shared over a period of years.

Much love, dear Peter,

MARION

Michael Tippett

'Remember your lovers' from *The Heart's Assurance* (1950–1). Words by Sidney Keyes
Autograph manuscript

Theodor Uppman

Back in California with Jean and our children after eight long months alone in New York attempting to establish a singing career, I reluctantly took a job in a factory. Within a month I was called to New York to audition for Billy Budd, and soon after, learning that I had been chosen for the role, was off to London. Following are excerpts from letters to Jean, who waited patiently in California with Margot and Michael.

London, 1951

This whole thing is still the loveliest fairytale imaginable. In New York on Tuesday I signed a contract with Columbia Artists Management. Wednesday I was interviewed for the Sunday *New York Times*. Thursday, hectic; borrowed $50, got my passport, went to say goodbye to Clytie Mundy; picked up fourth act of *Billy* which had just arrived; received word that Covent Garden contract had changes; rushed to discuss them and initial contract; taxied to hotel to pick up luggage and then to Waldorf for airport bus. Ticket, sent to Waldorf, was lost, and discovered just before bus left. Smooth flight; arrived on cold, drizzly afternoon in London. . . . Registered at the police station. No work permit yet, so can't rehearse at Covent Garden; will coach at home of one of the *répétiteurs*. Sunday, went to hear Ben Britten and Peter Pears do a beautiful concert at Victoria and Albert Museum. They had returned from France on Saturday. Went back to see them after; they recognized me from pictures before I introduced myself. . . . I've just returned from a long walk in Kensington Gardens – children shrieking with delight at swans and ducks in the Serpentine – kept thinking of you and Margot and Michael, and how much you would have loved it. . . . I've had no time for anything but work. Began blocking scenes with Peter Pears and others. Basil Coleman is the producer – a young, spirited and imaginative man. . . . After rehearsal went with Ben and Peter to their apartment to go through the score and talk over the character of Billy. Ben is an inspiration – what a genius, and yet so human and simple. He's unbelievably patient, and his wit and energy are a wonder. . . . First full dress rehearsal (piano only). It is more thrilling than I can ever say. The rumour that Krips would not conduct was confirmed, and Ben will conduct instead. Everyone is happy except Ben, who says he is absolutely petrified at the thought. I wish you could hear my final aria in the last act – some of the most beautiful music ever written. Peter is ideal as Vere. . . . Saturday's opening was the greatest thrill I've ever experienced on the stage. Everyone in the cast outdid himself. I'll never forget the wonderful feeling, and the cheers, bravos and stamping feet are still ringing in my ears.

And that, dear Peter, was only the beginning. Our lives have been enriched beyond all measure by your friendship. What more can Jean and I say than 'Peter Pears, God bless you!'

TED

William Walton

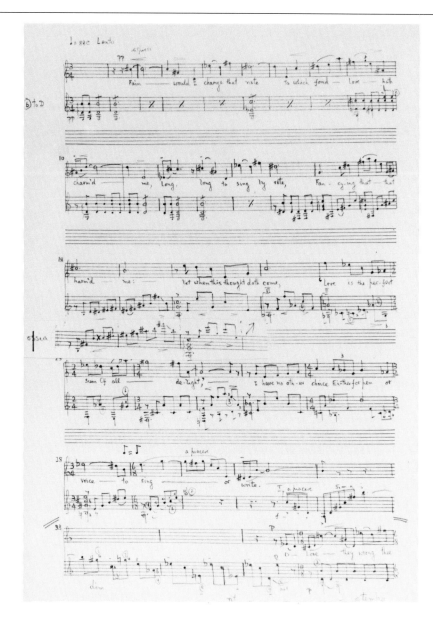

A page from *Anon in Love* (1959) Six songs for tenor and guitar.
Anonymous 16th/17th Century Lyrics. 'To L.S.' 'For Peter Pears and Julian Bream'.
Autograph manuscript

Fanny Waterman

Dear Peter,

I was privileged to sit next to you as a member of the jury for the last Mozart Competition in London, and I recall your sensitive reactions to the performances of the young players – your admiration and respect for the born artist, and your boredom with the mediocre.

Competitions have recently been under fire, but as you yourself have served on several juries, may I presume that you feel that competitions are of some worth? What do juries look for when they are listening to these young musicians? Beauty of tone, musical integrity, a fine technique, rhythmic vitality, understanding of the music's moods and, the most vital ingredient of all, that indefinable magic, which will appeal to Everyman and the musical connoisseur alike.

Murray Perahia, who won the first prize at the 1972 Leeds International Pianoforte Competition, has all these qualities. Immediately after the Competition, we all came down for one of your musical weekends at Aldeburgh, as it had been a lifelong dream of Murray's to meet you and Ben. He admired you both, and apart from his success in Leeds, his visit to Aldeburgh to meet you was, I believe, a highlight in his life.

Ben's piano playing was unique, and Murray's playing has to my mind many of the same magical qualities. It was surely fate, that after Ben's serious illness, Murray was to serve you in another memorable partnership.

Not only were you Ben's inspiration, but you have also inspired so many other musicians, who will be forever grateful to you.

Countless blessings on your 75th birthday – continue to enjoy your heavenly art and your friendships for many years to come.

Yours ever,

FANNY

Beth Welford

Dear Peter,

So you are going to be 75. I passed that age last June, it is not too bad!

I have been asked to contribute to some very secret something which is to be given to you, which of course I am so happy to do.

I am trying to remember when we first met. It must have been in 1937, probably in the flat I shared with Ben in Finchley Road, soon after Peter Burra was killed in that dreadful plane crash. Anyway I can recall the handsome young singer, being introduced to me. You were then with the BBC Singers I believe. Little did I think then how much a part of our lives you were to become.

Apart from all you did for and with Ben, I have always looked on you as a very dear 'other' brother.

Sadly, now you do not sing any more, but I have your voice on many records and tapes, so that I can still listen to your singing. Particularly when you are singing and Ben is playing is something that gives me so much pleasure, and now of course some sadness. Also all the roles you created in Ben's operas. I have been to most of them many times since you stopped singing, but there has never been anyone to sing or act them as you did. Always I say to myself, oh why can't it be Peter? This or that singer is no good, or not half as good.

The people of our generation are the fortunate ones, who have had the chance to see you in so many wonderful performances.

Thank you Peter for all you have given us.

With love from

BETH

Sir John Willis

My dear Peter,

I am very proud to be among your numerous friends and admirers to wish you many happy returns in the *Festschrift* to be presented to you on your 75th birthday. My only title to be included is that we have known each other since you came to Lancing in September 1923 as a classical scholar in a vintage year. Although I preceded you by only a year, you have always managed to remain two years younger than I. I had assumed that was because you looked that much younger, not that you came as a precocious barely 13-year-old. Do you remember Peter Pares in my house? His father was Professor of Russian at London University. His brother and cousin were in the house at the same time, so he had to be 'primus inter pares'. You, of course, were unique.

I think it was many years after Lancing before we met again, although your voice became increasingly familiar. Amy Nichol invited us to meet you and Ben soon after Barbara and I arrived in Snape twenty years ago. It has been wonderful for me to have renewed our old friendship, for us to have known Ben, and to have had the joy of your Festival.

It does not seem that five years have passed since I welcomed you to the Septuagenarians' Club. Though short to others much of them has been long and infinitely arduous for you. Your courage and determination in the face of your disabling illness have been an inspiration to all those who know and love you. May they sustain you long enough for your membership of the Octogenarians' Club to be acclaimed – perhaps even by me!

Yours affectionately,

JACK

Paul Wilson and the Staff of the
Britten–Pears Library

The Britten–Pears Library greets you, Peter.

Libraries and birthdays have a certain splendidly luxurious quality about them, don't you think? They both freeze time. Libraries, by slowly accumulating their stock-in-trade, sifting it, indexing it, conserving it, making it intelligible and available to the (non-paying) customers, create out of ephemera a permanent thing, unique and characteristic of its founders. Birthdays distil the actions and experiences of lives, giving us a moment to enjoy the best of them all over again.

You've given us and still give us several sorts of richness. Were it not for your wisdom and your knowledge of early printed vocal music we shouldn't have built up the huge collection that we have with its rarities and unique pieces. The *Monthly Mask of Vocal Music* sheets surpass all other collections, except possibly that of Harvard. The songs of the eighteenth-century pleasure gardens and theatres run into thousands, a marvellous conspectus. First and early editions of Byrd, Wilbye, Purcell, Boyce, Hook and Arne crowd in. Dibdin abounds. How pleasurable it is for librarian and student to show and be shown the first edition of the Schubert song that he or she (the student, that is!) will be singing at a masterclass that evening. How fascinating to see your handwriting amid the Britten manuscripts, taking a hand in the creation of scenarios of *Peter Grimes* and the libretto of *A Midsummer Night's Dream* and of so much more, and in the copying of music and words. Thank you for *your* manuscripts of Ben's music, thank you for *your* manuscripts of other composers' works and for *your* copies of the works you've sung and directed.

Virtually all our visitors – performers, writers, scholars, students – catch and remark on the feeling of serenity that is immanent in the Library. It's hard to pin down *why* they feel it but they *see* glints of Sickert's Venice and John Piper's Loxford and sense, quite justifiably, that the place is full of riches unguessed.

The riches are great (see above!), or endearing, or both. Some ninety tomes instruct us how to sing; a similar number of singers' biographies, autobiographies or ghost writings tell us in some detail how they *have* sung, Musingly, Memorially and, of course, on Wings! We do note a few lacunae however. Essex is a very fine county in its way but there is no *Suffolk Harmony*, a grievous lack. In the singers' corner I see that we jump from Patti to Sims Reeves. We look to you, our serene co-founder, to stop these gaps for us.

Meanwhile, a very Happy Birthday.

PAUL WILSON

Anne Wood

Dearest Peter,

So you are 75! I am two or three years older, and though my memory is not of the best, I remember clearly our first meetings when we were both in our twenties and my heart was won by the beauty of your young voice, your phrasing and your exquisite appreciation and delivery of the English language. Here, I thought, was the complete musician and so it proved. We went together through three years with the BBC Singers, far from wholly satisfying to us, but it provided a welcome weekly cheque. In due course we both left, you to America – your voice was growing and your musical life extending. The gaps in my memory yield up clear remembrances of wonderful early concerts and meetings with you and Ben and Marion and her mother and father and others. To that early period belongs my first London recital at the now extinct Grotrian Hall, at which, as you reminded me recently, I sang two of your songs. Happy memory! I think all of us who knew you then had the feel, the certainty, that here was something special and vastly important growing amongst us all.

And so it was of course, and still is. As I think about it all, dates get jumbled but 'occasions' remain crystal clear – you coming to sing to Iris and me on your final return from America, with your 'new' voice, stunning us with Italian operatic arias; hearing you in *Così* at the Cambridge Theatre along with Joan and Mab Ritchie, and in *The Bartered Bride* at Sadler's Wells – moments of glory in an exhausted world. And *Peter Grimes* – I got to the second performance in UNRRA uniform, straight from Belsen and the refugee camps of broken humanity in Germany. Unbelievable, it seemed, that here was growth and creation. A marvellous evening of healing to me and many others. Somewhere in time came two years for me as General Manager of the EOG, of going to Holland with you and being convulsed by your 'rendition' of a conversation in the Dutch language of which you knew not one word! And having the privilege of sharing a recital with you and Ben at the Aldeburgh Festival, of the Wolf

Italienische Lieder, and taking part with you in the first performance in England of the *Spring Symphony*. And listening to countless marvellous concerts of yours and Ben's.

So what makes your performances shine like beacons along the path of my musical life? The answer is clear – because you are an Illuminator. Not only have you, in your lifetime, opened up acres of buried or neglected English and other music, and at the other end of the time-scale, encouraged and commissioned a great deal of new music; but also you, together with Ben, have taken English music and English performances all over the world and have thus forged links with other peoples, including Russians, which will grow strong and flourish long after we are gone.

And now you pass on your lifetime of musical experience to the younger generation. So do I, in a much humbler way, and I suspect you enjoy, as I do, the feeling that one's past musical life spans a remarkable period, and that we even have something to offer to the future.

Very many happy returns, and much love,

ANNE

1. Peter Pears aged 4 or 5.

2. Uncle Peter (aged 11) with his first niece.

3. Lancing College chamber music groups c. 1927.
   Behind the pianist (Peter Pears) stands Peter Burra.

4. In the gardens at Glyndebourne, 1938.
   (from a group photograph of members of the chorus)

5. A publicity photograph c. 1940.

Peter Pears: A Collage up to the age of thirty

BENJAMIN BRITTEN
FROM HIS PERSONAL DIARIES
FOR 1937 AND 1938

Selected and minimally annotated by Donald Mitchell

1937

Friday, 30 April

I have a rehearsal with Boult of H.F. [*Our Hunting Fathers*] at BBC at 11.30 – it goes quite well, tho' he doesn't really grasp the work – tho' he is marvellously painstaking. Sophie [Wyss] of course sings well. Lunch after with her & Arnold jun. [her son: her husband was Arnold Gyde], & John & Millicent Francis. Then I meet Poppy Vulliamy & have long talks with her. She goes off to Spain very soon to look after the evacuated children from Madrid & Malaga. I have agreed to adopt one & pay for him for a year. Back here in aft. & then out to dinner with Peter Piers [*sic*: BB was a notoriously faulty speller and in these early days had not yet mastered the correct spelling of PP's name] & Basil Douglas – very nice, but sad as we have to discuss what is best about Peter Burra's things. [Peter Burra (1909–1937), a gifted and close schoolfriend of PP, had tragically died in an air accident on 27 April: he was a passenger in a plane which crashed near Bucklebury Common, Berkshire. Burra wrote on art, music and literature. His admirable essay on Forster's *A Passage to India* appears as an introduction to the Everyman edition of the novel. See also entries below.]

Thursday, 6 May

[. . .]*

After dinner general slack & then Kit [Welford, later husband of BB's sister, Beth] drops me at Paddington at 10.45 & I meet Peter Pears [NB!] & travel with him in a packed dirty train to Reading where we arrive about mid-night – & set out for the Behrends' house (Burclere) [*recte* Burghclere; Mr and Mrs J.L. Behrend (see also George Behrend, their son, pp. 8–9) were well-known patrons of art, friendds of PP and Burra] on his motor-bike, & the pouring, pouring rain. After wandering helplessly in the maze of roads over the common – very cold & damp to our skins – & me pretty sore behind, being unused to pillion riding – we knock up people in the only house with a light we meet at all, & get some rather vague instructions from them. Wander further & quite by accident alight on the house – at about 1.45 or 50. Have hot baths & straight to bed. The Behrends themselves are in town.

---

* Editorial omission.

Friday, 7 May

After a 9 o'clock breakfast Peter & I go over to Peter Burra's house (Foxhold) to spend day sorting out letters, photos & other personalities [*sic*: personalia?] preparatory to the big clear up to take place soon. Peter Pears is a dear & a very sympathetic person. – tho' I'll admit I am not too keen on travelling on his motor-bike!
[. . .]

Wednesday, 26 May

Work at a new song in the morning & a little in the afternoon – by W.H.A. [W. H. Auden: this would have been one of the settings for *On this Island*] – middle is bad tho' beginning & end good. Ronald Duncan & I have lunch at Dutch Oven – it is good to see him; & we exchange miseries & revel in Schadenfreude.

After dinner Peter Pears gives me a ticket for & I go with him to the first of the London Musical Festival BBC. orch. concerts with Toscanini. He certainly is a first-rate man – not always perhaps absolutely as one feels the works – but so marvellously efficient & sensitive with the orchestra – like no one else. The Busoni Rondo Arlecchinesco was electrifying (a grand work – perhaps Busoni's musical invention didn't always equal his ideas) – the Daphnis & Chloe was a revelation; it can never have sounded like that before – all the colours melted into each other, & never was the colour all important. Coriolan – great – & Brahms' 1st was as good as it could be – but it is a very bad work – desperately ugly & pretentious & not redeemed by its several good patches. But the Beethoven stood out from all by its colossal welding [of] inspiration, technique, & philosophy. One of the number one works of the world.

Peter is a dear.

Friday, 10 September

Before Peter leaves in the morning he runs thro' my Emily Brontë song (for Michaelmas programme) [a BBC radio feature: *The Company of Heaven*] that he's going to sing – & he makes it sound charming. He is a good singer & a first-rate musician.
[. . .]

Friday, 15 October

Busy packing & things – after dinner Lennox B. [Berkeley] & Christopher Isherwood come to coffee to hear Peter sing my new songs [*On this Island*] & are considerably pleased – as I admit I am. Peter sings them well – if he studies he will be a very good singer. He's certainly one of the nicest people I know, but frightfully reticent.

1938

Friday, 28 January

Spend day flat-hunting (without success) with Peter.
[. . .]

Thursday, 3 February

Spend day flat-hunting (lunch with Frank B. [Bridge] at Kensington).
[. . .]

Friday, 4 February

Business in morning (mostly at Booseys with Ralph [Hawkes]) – & after lunch
Peter and I do a bit more flat-hunting (still unsuccessful).
[. . .]

Friday, 11 February

More hopeless flat-hunting in morning – & then in aft. I leave Peter to it, & come
back with Mrs Welford in car to Peasenhall arr. about 8.0.
[. . .]

Friday, 18 February

Up by mid-day train – then in afternoon Peter & I see a flat, about the 100th I
should think – but it's no good.
[. . .]

Friday, 25 February

In morning Peter & I sign up a flat – [43] Nevern Square – Dick Wood's late
place. [It was for Richard Wood, Anne Wood's brother and, like her, a professional singer, that BB was later to write (while Wood was a prisoner of war) *The
Ballad of Little Musgrave and Lady Barnard.*] 2 very nice rooms. Probably a rash
decision, but we *must* get settled. [. . .] See 5.0 the first full-length Disney
'Snow White' – grand entertainment & some terrific incidents.

I'm staying with Peter. See Flat in morning & then I go up to lunch with Easdales. [Brian Easdale was musical director of the Group Theatre. His opera, *The Sleeping Children*, was to be commissioned by the English Opera Group and performed in 1951.]
[. . .]

Friday, 4 March

Early up, & see Peter off to Prague.
[. . .]

Saturday, 12 March

[. . .]
Hitler marches into Austria, rumour has it that Czecho.S. & Russia have mobilised – so what! War within a month at least, I suppose & end to all this pleasure – end of Snape, end of Concerto [the Piano Concerto, on which BB was working at this time], friends, work, love – oh, blast, blast, damn . . .

Monday, 14 March

[. . .]
Peter's back from Prague – safely, but with grim news of Germany under Nazi rule.

Tuesday, 15 March

Peter's furniture is moved into flat.
[. . .]

Wednesday, 16 March

Lunch with Beth at Easdales. Furniture is moved after. To-night we sleep at flat – unfurnished a bit still, but going to be grand I think. Eat in.

PETER:
THE ARTIST IN
PERFORMANCE

Peter Pears: Roles in operas by *composers other than* Benjamin Britten

Peter Pears: Roles in operas by *Benjamin Britten*

115

Peter Pears: Roles in operas by *composers other than* Benjamin Britten

1. As Satyavan, with Arda Mandikian as Savitri and Thomas Hemsley (standing) as Death in EOG production of Holst's *Savitri* at the Aldeburgh Festival, 1956.

2. As Ferrando (left) with John Hargreaves as Guglielmo in Mozart's *Così Fan Tutte* at the Prince's Theatre, London, 1944. (Sadler's Wells Opera Company production).

3. As Idomeneo in EOG production of Mozart's *Idomeneo* at the Aldeburgh Festival, 1969.

4. As The Husband with Jennifer Vyvyan as his wife in EOG production of Poulenc's *Les Mamelles de Tirésias* at the Aldeburgh Festival, 1958.

5. As Vašek (centre) in the Royal Opera House production of Smetana's *The Bartered Bride*, 1955, with Adèle Leigh (Esmeralda) and David Tree (Circus master).

6. As Alfredo in Verdi's *La Traviata* (Sadler's Wells Opera Company production, 1943).

7. As David (left) in Wagner's *The Mastersingers of Nuremberg* (in English) at the Royal Opera House, Covent Garden, 1957, with Erich Witte as Walther von Stolzing.

8. As Pandarus with Magda Laszlo as Cressida in the original production of Walton's *Troilus and Cressida* at the Royal Opera House, Covent Garden, December 1954.

Peter Pears: Roles in operas by *Benjamin Britten*.

1. Peter Grimes, in the original production at Sadler's Wells. June 1949.

2. Male Chorus and Female Chorus (Joan Cross) in the first production of *The Rape of Lucretia*, Glyndebourne, July 1946.

3. Albert Herring, in the original EOG production of the opera at Glyndebourne, June 1947.

4. Captain Macheath and Polly Peachum (Nancy Evans) in Britten's realization of *The Beggar's Opera*, the original EOG production at the Arts Theatre, Cambridge, May 1948. *Photo*: Maria Austria.

5. *Billy Budd*: Royal Opera House, Covent Garden, December 1951. Mr. Redburn (Hervey Alan – centre) presides at the court of inquiry, aided by Mr. Flint (Geraint Evans). Captain Vere gives evidence.

6. *The Turn of the Screw*: the EOG's production at Stratford, Ontario, August 1957. The two ghosts, Peter Quint and Miss Jessel (Arda Mandikian).

7. The Church Operas at Orford: *The Burning Fiery Furnace*, June 1966. The Astrologer (Bryan Drake) speaks persuasively to Misael (Robert Tear), Ananias (John Shirley-Quirk) and Azarias (Victor Godfrey) as Nebuchadnezzar watches.

8. *Owen Wingrave* B.B.C. Television, 16th May 1971.
Owen's grandfather, General Sir Philip Wingrave.

9. *Death in Venice*: EOG production at the Maltings, Snape, 16th June 1973.
The Hotel Barber (John Shirley-Quirk) attends to Gustav von Aschenbach.

PETER PEARS IN OPERA

Harold Rosenthal

What other singer in operatic history has created fourteen roles in operas specially composed for him – twelve by one composer? What other tenor has there been who made his first appearance at the Metropolitan Opera in New York when he was in his mid-sixties? And what other tenor made his début at Glyndebourne in a silent role? The tenor in question is, of course, Peter Pears, whose operatic career, as can be seen from the list below, has been most impressive, beginning as it did while he was still a student at the Royal College of Music in London, when he sang Belmonte in *Die Entführung aus dem Serail* and, soon after, a small role in Delius's *A Village Romeo and Juliet* conducted by Beecham.

Peter Pears's career has been very special, closely connected with the operatic output of Benjamin Britten, the composer who wrote twelve roles for him – fourteen if one includes Britten's realizations of *The Beggar's Opera* and *Dido and Aeneas* (in which he shared the role of Aeneas with Bruce Boyce).

I first heard Peter Pears in the summer of 1943, when on leave from the army. I spent night after night at the New Theatre in St Martin's Lane, which was the home of the London seasons of Sadler's Wells Opera during the war. I can still recollect vividly the pleasure this 'new' tenor gave me, which resulted in my taking every opportunity I could to hear him: as the Duke of Mantua in *Rigoletto*, Almaviva in *The Barber of Seville* – hilariously funny, disguised as Alonzo giving Rosina (Rose Hill) her music lesson – Alfredo in *La Traviata*, as Tamino, as Vašek in *The Bartered Bride*, and as many performances as I could manage of *Così fan tutte* in which he sang Ferrando (the cast was Joan Cross, Margaret Ritchie – later Anna Pollak, Rose Hill, John Hargreaves and Owen Brannigan).

Then came the night that changed English operatic history, the first *Peter Grimes* at the reopened Sadler's Wells Theatre, on 7 June 1945. 'Mr Peter Pears commanded all the vocal resources required for a great and exacting part' wrote *The Times*; while Scott Goddard in the *News Chronicle* wrote, 'Peter Pears as Grimes gave a profoundly sympathetic rendering of the part for which he will be remembered. Singing and acting were of one piece, and intensely moving.'

What for me have been the hallmarks of Peter Pears as an opera singer? The fact that he sang all his roles with an elegance and style rare among opera singers, and with a natural feeling for the music and especially for the text. His voice, a highly individual one, recognizable as soon as he has sung a single phrase, has always been at the service of the musician, and, more important, of the composer himself.

When once asked what roles he regretted he had never sung, he replied Werther and the title role in Pfitzner's *Palestrina*. This latter opera was one in which the great Julius Patzak (surely the German equivalent of Peter Pears) was unsurpassed. Another of the roles, as we can hear on records, in which Patzak was unique was Loge in *Das Rheingold*; and that is the role more than any other that I wish Peter could have taken into his repertory.

This list does not include the many tours in Europe with the English Opera Group, or repeat performances of a number of operas.

1934	Royal College of Music, London. Belmonte in *Die Entführung aus dem Serail*; Ferrando in *Così fan tutte*; Poor Horn-Player in *A Village Romeo and Juliet*.
1936–8	While member of the BBC Singers took part in several concert and studio performances of opera, including the Second Foreman in the first performance in England of *Lady Macbeth of Mtsensk* (Queen's Hall, March 1936) under Albert Coates; and one of the Students of Wittenberg in first performance in England of Busoni's *Doctor Faust* (Queen's Hall, March 1937) under Adrian Boult.
1938	Glyndebourne. Member of chorus including 'walk-on' part in Verdi's *Macbeth* (Duncan) and Major-Domo in *Don Pasquale*.
1942	Strand Theatre, London. Title role in *The Tales of Hoffmann* (sharing role with Henry Wendon).
1943–5	Joins Sadler's Wells Opera remaining until 1945 and singing: Almaviva (*The Barber of Seville*), Duke of Mantua, Tamino, Ferrando, Alfredo (*La Traviata*), Rodolfo and Vašek, and finally creating Peter Grimes when company returned to Rosebery Avenue on 7 June 1945.
1946	Zürich Opera. Grimes.
1946	Glyndebourne. Creates Male Chorus in *The Rape of Lucretia*.
1947	Glyndebourne. Creates title role in *Albert Herring*.
1948	English Opera Group. Macheath in *The Beggar's Opera*. Grimes at Covent Garden (also in 1948–9, 1953–4, 1957–8 and 1962–3).
1951	EOG. Narrator in *Il combattimento di Tancredi e Clorinda*; Aeneas in *Dido and Aeneas*. Covent Garden. Tamino (under Kleiber) and creates Captain Vere in *Billy Budd* (1 December 1951).

Cologne. Title role in *Oedipus Rex*, taped performance (recorded), conducted by Stravinsky (October).

1952   Aldeburgh. Hawthorne in *Love in a Village*.

1953   Covent Garden. Creates Essex in *Gloriana* (8 June 1953).

1954   Venice, La Fenice. Creates Quint in *The Turn of the Screw* (with EOG).
        Covent Garden. Creates Pandarus in Walton's *Troilus and Cressida*.

1955   Covent Garden. Vašek in new production of *The Bartered Bride*.

1956   Aldeburgh. Satyavan in Holst's *Savitri* (and subsequently with EOG on tour).
        Creates Boaz in Lennox Berkeley's *Ruth* at Scala Theatre, London, in EOG's season.

1957   Covent Garden. Sings David in new production of *The Mastersingers of Nuremberg*.

1958   Aldeburgh. Husband in Poulenc's *Les Mamelles de Tirésias*.

1960   Aldeburgh. Creates Flute in *A Midsummer Night's Dream*.

1964   Aldeburgh. Creates Madwoman in *Curlew River*.
        Tours USSR with EOG.

1966   Aldeburgh. Creates Nebuchadnezzar in *The Burning Fiery Furnace*.

1968   Aldeburgh. Creates the Tempter in *The Prodigal Son*.

1969   Aldeburgh. Sings first Idomeneo.

1971   BBC Television. Creates Sir Philip in *Owen Wingrave* (subsequently on stage at Covent Garden in May 1973).

1973   Aldeburgh (Snape). Creates Aschenbach in *Death in Venice* (subsequently seen at Covent Garden and Metropolitan, New York).
        Records the Emperor Altoum in *Turandot* for Decca.

1974   New York. Makes Met début as Aschenbach.

1978   New York. Met. Sings Captain Vere.
        London, Covent Garden. Sings Aschenbach again at Covent Garden Prom (March 31) and makes his last Covent Garden appearance in role on April 11.

1979   Aldeburgh. Sings Monsieur Triquet in *Eugene Onegin*.
        Edinburgh Festival. Sings Prologue in *The Turn of the Screw* (last stage appearance).

February 1980. A performance of Schumann's *Dichterliebe* at the Royal Scottish Academy of Music and Drama, Glasgow.

THE FIRST PERFORMANCES

The Archivists of the Britten–Pears Library

We have attempted to list here all those works of which Peter Pears gave the first performance, or in whose premières he took part. In a project of this kind – which is designed to be a surprise to its dedicatee – one has an insoluble problem from the start: how can everything be discovered when questions cannot be asked of the one person who would be able to help? All the same, we hope that any composer who has been inadequately represented or inadvertently left out altogether will understand the dilemma and forgive the omission, applauding with the rest of us Peter's constantly encouraging enthusiasm for presenting and promoting the works of all those contemporary composers who have been fortunate enough to write for him.

Works premièred by the BBC Singers while Peter Pears was singing with them have not been included, nor have any stage premières of that pre-war period in which he may have sung. And although many of Benjamin Britten's realizations of songs by Purcell and his contemporaries were written for PP to sing, these and the Britten Folk Song Arrangements (likewise mostly made for their joint recital programmes) have been omitted.

SOLO VOICE(S) WITH PIANO (OR ONE OTHER INSTRUMENT) OR UNACCOMPANIED

David Bedford   *Because he liked to be at home*
for tenor (with treble recorder) and harp, text by Kenneth Patchen
The Maltings, Snape, 19 June 1974, with Osian Ellis

Richard Rodney Bennett   *Three Songs*
for unaccompanied tenor voice, text by José Garcia Villa

Richard Rodney Bennett   *Tom o'Bedlam's Song*
for tenor and cello
National Gallery of Scotland, Edinburgh, 29 November 1961, with Joan Dickson

Lennox Berkeley   *Five Herrick Songs*, Op. 89
for tenor and harp
The Maltings, Snape, 19 June 1974, with Osian Ellis

Lennox Berkeley *Four Ronsard Sonnets*, Op. 40
for two tenors and piano 1952, with Hugues Cuénod
and (revised version)
The Maltings, Snape, 14 June 1978, with Ian Partridge and Steuart Bedford

Lennox Berkeley *Songs of the Half-light*, Op. 65
for voice and guitar, texts by Walter de la Mare
Jubilee Hall, Aldeburgh, 22 June 1965, with Julian Bream

James Bernard *Shepherd's Warning*
pastoral song-cycle for voice and guitar, text by Paul Dehn
Wigmore Hall, 12 November 1954, with Julian Bream

Benjamin Britten *A Birthday Hansel*, Op. 92
for voice and harp, text by Robert Burns
Cardiff, 19 March 1976, with Osian Ellis (first public performance)

Benjamin Britten *Canticle I*, Op. 40, 'My Beloved is Mine'
for high voice and piano, text by Francis Quarles
Dick Sheppard Memorial Concert, Central Hall, Westminster, 1 November 1947,
with Benjamin Britten

Benjamin Britten *Canticle II*, Op. 51, Abraham and Isaac
for alto and tenor voices and piano, text from the Chester Miracle Play
Nottingham, 21 January 1952, with Kathleen Ferrier and Benjamin Britten

Benjamin Britten *Canticle IV*, Op. 84, Journey of the Magi
for counter-tenor, tenor and baritone voices and piano, text by T. S. Eliot
The Maltings, Snape, 26 June 1971,
with James Bowman, John Shirley-Quirk and Benjamin Britten

Benjamin Britten *Canticle V*, Op. 89, The Death of Saint Narcissus
for tenor and harp, text by T. S. Eliot
Schloss Elmau, 15 January 1975, with Osian Ellis

Benjamin Britten *The Holy Sonnets of John Donne*, Op. 35
for high voice and piano
Wigmore Hall, 22 November 1945, with Benjamin Britten

Benjamin Britten *Sechs Hölderlin-Fragmente*, Op. 61
for voice and piano
Schloss Wolfsgarten, 20 November 1958, with Benjamin Britten

Benjamin Britten *Seven Sonnets of Michelangelo*, Op. 22
for tenor and piano
Wigmore Hall, 23 September 1942, with Benjamin Britten

Benjamin Britten *Songs from the Chinese*, Op. 58
for high voice and guitar, texts by Chinese poets (translated by Arthur Waley)
Great Glemham House, 17 June 1958, with Julian Bream

Benjamin Britten *Who are these children?*, Op. 84
for tenor and piano, texts by William Soutar
National Gallery of Scotland, 4 May 1971, with Benjamin Britten

Benjamin Britten   *Winter Words*, Op. 52
for high voice and piano, texts by Thomas Hardy
Harewood House, 8 October 1953, with Benjamin Britten

Alan Bush   *Voices of the Prophets*
cantata for tenor and piano, texts from various sources
Royal Festival Hall, London, 22 May 1953, with Noel Mewton-Wood

Aaron Copland   *Five Old American Songs*
arranged for tenor and piano
Jubilee Hall, Aldeburgh, 18 June 1950, with Benjamin Britten

Arnold Cooke   *This Worldes Joie*
for unaccompanied tenor voice, to text of *c*.1300
Parish Church, Aldeburgh, 24 June 1955

Gordon Crosse   *The Cool Web*, Op. 36
for tenor and piano, texts by Stevie Smith
The Maltings, Snape, 16 June 1975, with Clifford Benson

Richard Drakeford   *Songs of Thomas Wyatt*
for unaccompanied tenor voice
Parish Church, Little Missenden, Bucks., October 1975

Peter Racine Fricker   *O Mistress Mine*
for tenor and guitar, text by Shakespeare
Dartington Hall, 31 July 1962, with Julian Bream

Robin Holloway   *This is just to say*
song cycle for tenor and piano, texts by William Carlos Williams
Jubilee Hall, Aldeburgh, 16 June 1977, with Stephen Ralls

Robin Holloway   *Willow Cycle*, Op. 35, No. 2
for tenor and harp, to sixteenth-century texts
Jubilee Hall, Aldeburgh, 23 June 1978, with Osian Ellis

Robin Holloway   *La Figlia che Piange*
for tenor and harp, text by T. S. Eliot
The Maltings, Snape, 9 June 1979, with Osian Ellis

Jørgen Jersild   *Puzzle from Wonderland*
for tenor and harp, text by Lewis Carroll
The Maltings, Snape, 17 June 1976, with Osian Ellis

Elizabeth Maconchy   *Three Songs*
for tenor and harp, with texts by Shelley, Byron and Thomas Campbell
The Maltings, Snape, 19 June 1974, with Osian Ellis

Elizabeth Maconchy   *Hymn to God the Father*
for tenor and piano, text by John Donne
Jubilee Hall, Aldeburgh, 22 June 1965, with Viola Tunnard

Colin Matthews   *Five Sonnets: To Orpheus*
for tenor and harp, texts by Rainer Maria Rilke
Wigmore Hall, 1 June 1977, with Osian Ellis

Colin Matthews   *Shadows in the Water*
for tenor and piano, text by Thomas Traherne
The Maltings, Snape, 11 June 1980, with Steuart Bedford

Thea Musgrave   *Ballad: Sir Patrick Spens*
for tenor and guitar
Great Glemham House, Suffolk, 7 July 1961, with Julian Bream

Arne Nordheim   *To One Singing*
for tenor and harp, text by Shelley
The Maltings, Snape, 17 June 1976, with Osian Ellis

Arthur Oldham   *Five Chinese Lyrics*
for tenor and piano, translated by Arthur Waley and Helen Waddell
Jubilee Hall, Aldeburgh, 19 June 1949, with Benjamin Britten

Arthur Oldham   *The Commandment of Love*
for tenor and piano, text by Richard Rolle
Jubilee Hall, Aldeburgh, 13 June 1951, with Benjamin Britten

Arthur Oldham   *The Sunne Rising*
for tenor and piano, text by John Donne
Wigmore Hall, 24 April 1948, with Benjamin Britten

Thomas Pitfield   *Winter Song*
for tenor and piano, text by Katherine Mansfield
Fyvie Hall, London Polytechnic, 4 January 1944, with Benjamin Britten

Priaulx Rainier   *(Cycle for) Declamation*
for unaccompanied tenor voice, text by John Donne
Parish Church, Aldeburgh, 25 June 1953

Priaulx Rainier   *Prayers from the Ark*
for tenor and harp, texts by Rumer Godden from the French
of Carmen Bernos de Gasztold
Queen Elizabeth Hall, 14 January 1976, with Osian Ellis

Alan Ridout   *On Heliodora*
for unaccompanied tenor voice, to three poems of Meleagros
Wigmore Hall, 16 December 1960

Stig Schonberg   *O Sag*
for tenor and harp, text by Gosta Norell
The Maltings, Snape, 17 June 1976, with Osian Ellis

Gary Schurmann   *Five Facets*
for tenor and piano, text by F. Sybrand Bijlsma
Wigmore Hall, 20 January 1946, with Benjamin Britten

Mátyás Seiber   *To Poetry*
song-cycle for tenor and piano, texts by various authors
Royal Festival Hall, 22 May 1953, with Noel Mewton-Wood

Ronald Stevenson   *Border Boyhood*
for tenor and piano, texts by Hugh MacDiarmid
Jubilee Hall, Aldeburgh, 16 June 1971, with Ronald Stevenson

Ronald Stevenson *Nine Haiku*
for tenor and harp, texts by Japanese poets, translated by Keith Bosley
West Linton, Peeblesshire, October 1975, with Osian Ellis

Michael Tippett *Boyhood's End*
cantata for tenor and piano, text by W. H. Hudson
Leicester Art Gallery, 29 July 1943, with Benjamin Britten

Michael Tippett *The Heart's Assurance*
for high voice and piano, texts by Alun Lewis and Sidney Keyes
Wigmore Hall, 7 May 1951, with Benjamin Britten

Michael Tippett *Songs for Achilles*
for voice and guitar, texts by the composer
Great Glemham House, Suffolk, 7 July 1961, with Julian Bream

William Walton *Anon in Love*
six songs for tenor and guitar, to anonymous texts
Shrubland Park, Claydon, Suffolk, 21 June 1960, with Julian Bream

Egon Wellesz *Alleluia Dic Nobis*
for unaccompanied tenor voice, tenth-century text
1958

Malcolm Williamson *Ay Flattering Fortune*
for unaccompanied tenor voice, text by Sir Thomas More
Parish Church, Aldeburgh, 24 June 1955

R. W. Wood *Sonnet No. 64, Sonnet d'Automne, Epitaph*
for tenor and piano, texts by Shakespeare, Baudelaire and E. B. Browning
Fyvie Hall, London Polytechnic, 4 January 1944, with Benjamin Britten

William Wordsworth *The Snowflake*
for tenor and piano, text by Walter de la Mare
Fyvie Hall, London Polytechnic, 4 January 1944, with Benjamin Britten

SOLO VOICE(S) AND CHAMBER ENSEMBLE

David Bedford *On the Beach at Night*
for two tenors, piano (two and four hands) and chamber organ
The Maltings, Snape, 14 June 1978, with Ian Partridge, tenor, Steuart Bedford and
Graham Barber, keyboards

David Bedford *The Tentacles of the Dark Nebula*
for tenor and chamber ensemble, text by Arthur C. Clarke
Queen Elizabeth Hall, 22 September 1969, with the London Sinfonietta conducted by
David Atherton

Arthur Bliss *Elegiac Sonnet* in memory of Noel Mewton-Wood
for tenor, string quartet and piano, text by C. Day Lewis
Wigmore Hall, 28 January 1955, with the Zorian Quartet and Benjamin Britten, piano

Benjamin Britten *Canticle III*, Op. 55, Still Falls the Rain
for tenor voice, horn and piano, text by Edith Sitwell
Wigmore Hall, 28 January 1955, with Dennis Brain, horn, and Benjamin Britten

Sebastian Forbes *Death's Dominion*
song-cycle for tenor, flute, clarinet, string trio and piano, texts by Michael Langenheim
Jubilee Hall, Aldeburgh, 16 June 1971, with members of the English Chamber Orchestra

Peter Racine Fricker *Cantata*, Op. 37
for tenor and chamber ensemble, text by William Saroyan
Jubilee Hall, Aldeburgh, 21 June 1962, with members of the English Chamber Orchestra

Hans Werner Henze *Chamber Music 1958*
for tenor, guitar, clarinet, horn and string quintet, text by Hölderlin/Waeblinger
Hamburg, November 1958, with Julian Bream, guitar, and others

Robin Holloway *Moments of Vision*
cycle for speaker and four players, texts by various authors
The Maltings, Snape, 22 June 1984, with the Hartley Trio and John Evans (percussion)

Krzysztof Meyer *Lyric Triptych*, Op. 38
for tenor and chamber orchestra, texts by W. H. Auden
The Maltings, Snape, 22 June 1978, with Contrapuncti, conducted by Michael Lankester

Witold Lutoslawski *Paroles Tissées*
for tenor, strings, piano and percussion, texts by Jean-François Chabrun
Jubilee Hall, Aldeburgh, 20 June 1965, with Philomusica of London, conducted by
the composer

Robin Orr *Four Romantic Songs*
for tenor, oboe and string quartet, texts by Helen Waddell
The Friends House, London, 14 November 1950, with members of the
London Harpsichord Ensemble

Priaulx Rainier *The Bee Oracles*
for tenor, flute, oboe, violin, cello and harpsichord, texts by Edith Sitwell
Jubilee Hall, Aldeburgh, 17 June 1970, with the London Oboe Quartet and
Alan Harverson

Mátyás Seiber *Three Fragments* from 'A Portrait of the Artist as a Young Man'
Chamber cantata for speaker, chorus and eight instruments, text by James Joyce
Jubilee Hall, Aldeburgh, 25 June 1959, with the Dorian Singers and members of the
Melos Ensemble, conducted by the composer (first performance in UK)

John Tavener *Six Abbassid Songs*
for tenor, three flutes and percussion, sixth–eighth-century texts
The Maltings, Snape, 18 June 1980, with Jonathan Snowden, Julian Coward, Graham
Nash, flutes, and Ann Collis, percussion

William Walton *Façade II*
a further entertainment for reciter and chamber ensemble, texts by Edith Sitwell
The Maltings, Snape, 19 June 1979, with members of the English Chamber Orchestra,
conducted by Steuart Bedford (first complete performance)

Grace Williams (arr.) *Three Traditional Welsh Ballads*
for tenor, flute, oboe and string quartet
The Friends House, London, 14 November 1950, with members of the
London Harpsichord Ensemble

Douglas Young *Landscapes and Absences*
for tenor, cor anglais and string trio, text by T. S. Eliot
Wigmore Hall, 17 December 1972, with the London Oboe Quartet

VOICE(S) AND ORCHESTRA

solo voice

Lennox Berkeley *Four Ronsard Sonnets*, Op. 62
for tenor and orchestra
Royal Albert Hall, 9 August 1963, with the BBC Symphony Orchestra conducted by
the composer

Benjamin Britten *Nocturne*, Op. 60
for tenor voice, seven obligato instruments and string orchestra, texts by various poets
Leeds Town Hall, 16 October 1958, with the BBC Symphony Orchestra conducted by
Rudolph Schwartz

Benjamin Britten *Serenade*, Op. 31
for tenor solo, horn and strings, texts by various poets
Wigmore Hall, 15 October 1943, with Dennis Brain, horn, and string ensemble conducted
by Walter Goehr

Vagn Holmboe *Ballad*
tor tenor and orchestra, text by William Beattie
The Maltings, Snape, 9 June 1972, with the English Chamber Orchestra, conducted by
David Atherton

Arne Nordheim *Doria*
for tenor and orchestra, text by Ezra Pound
The Maltings, Snape, 16 June 1976, with the English Chamber Orchestra, conducted by
Steuart Bedford

Rolf Urs Ringger *Shelley Songs*
for tenor and orchestra
Zürich, 28 May 1980, with the Collegium Musicum, conducted by Paul Sacher

choral works, with soloists

Lennox Berkeley *Stabat Mater*, Op. 28
for six solo voices, and chamber orchestra, to thirteenth-century text
Zürich, August 1947, with members of the English Opera Group, conducted by
Benjamin Britten

Lennox Berkeley *Variations on a Hymn of Orlando Gibbons*, Op. 35
for tenor, chorus, strings and organ
Parish Church, Aldeburgh, 21 June 1952, with the Aldeburgh Festival Choir and
Orchestra, and Ralph Downes, organ, conducted by the composer

Benjamin Britten *Cantata Academica*, Carmen Basiliense, Op. 62
for S A T B solos, chorus and orchestra, Latin text compiled by Bernhard Wyss from the
charter of Basle University, etc.
Basle University, 1 July 1960, with Agnes Giebel, Elsa Cavelti, Heinz Rehfuss and the
Basler Kammerorchester, conducted by Paul Sacher

Benjamin Britten *Cantata Misericordium*, Op. 69
for tenor and baritone solos, small chorus and orchestra, Latin text by Patrick Wilkinson
Geneva, 1 September 1963, with Dietrich Fischer-Dieskau, le Motet de Genève and
l'Orchestre da la Suisse Romande conducted by Ernest Ansermet

Benjamin Britten *Saint Nicolas*, Op. 42
Cantata for tenor solo, chorus, semi-chorus, four boy singers and orchestra, text by
Eric Crozier
Parish Church, Aldeburgh, 5 June 1948, with the Aldeburgh Festival Chorus and
Orchestra, conducted by Leslie Woodgate

Benjamin Britten *Spring Symphony*, Op. 44
for S A T solos, chorus, boys' choiir and orchestra, texts by various poets and dramatists
Amsterdam, 14 July 1949, with Jo Vincent, Kathleen Ferrier, the Dutch Radio Chorus and
the Concertgebouw Orchestra conducted by Eduard van Beinum

Benjamin Britten *War Requiem*, Op. 66
for S T B solos, chorus, orchestra, chamber orchestra, boys' choir and organ, text: the
Missa pro Defunctis and poems by Wilfred Owen
St Michael's Cathedral, Coventry, 30 May 1962, with Heather Harper and Dietrich
Fischer-Dieskau, Coventry Festival Chorus etc., City of Birmingham Symphony
Orchestra and the Melos Ensemble, conducted by Meredith Davies and the composer

Bertus van Lier *The Song of Songs*
for S T B soloists, chamber choir and chamber orchestra
Oude Kerk, Amsterdam, 12 July 1949, with Dora van Doorn-Lindeman, Hermann Schey
and the Amsterdam Chamber Music Society, conducted by the composer

Michael Tippett *A Child of our Time*
oratorio for S A T B soloists, chorus and orchestra
Royal Adelphi Theatre, London, 19 March 1944, with Joan Cross, Margaret McArthur,
Norman Walker, the London Region Civil Defence and Morley College Choirs, the
London Philharmonic Orchestra conducted by Walter Goehr

VOCAL ENSEMBLE OR (UNACCOMPANIED) CHORUS WITH OR WITHOUT SOLOISTS

Lennox Berkeley *Crux Fidelis*, Op. 43
motet for tenor solo and chorus
Victoria and Albert Museum, 6 March 1955, with the Purcell Singers, conducted by
Imogen Holst

Benjamin Britten *A.M.D.G.* (1939)
for unaccompanied mixed voices, texts by Gerard Manley Hopkins
(end of 1939, in USA, with the Round Table Singers)

Benjamin Britten *Sacred and Profane*, Op. 91 Eight Medieval Lyrics for unaccompanied voices (S S A T B)
The Maltings, Snape, 14 September 1975
The Wilbye Consort, directed by Peter Pears

Benjamin Britten *A Wedding Anthem*, Op. 46
for soprano and tenor solos, choir and organ, text by Ronald Duncan
St Mark's, North Audley Street, 29 September 1949, with Joan Cross and the choir of
St Mark's conducted by the composer

Priaulx Rainier *Requiem*
for tenor solo and chorus, text by David Gascoyne
Victoria and Albert Museum, 15 April 1956, with the Purcell Singers, conducted by
Imogen Holst

OPERATIC ROLES

in works by contemporary composers

Lennox Berkeley *Ruth*, Op. 50
Libretto by Eric Crozier
Scala Theatre, London, 2 October 1956, with the English Opera Group, conducted by
Charles Mackerras
As Boaz

Benjamin Britten *Albert Herring*, Op. 39
Libretto by Eric Crozier
Glyndebourne, 20 June 1947, with the English Opera Group, conducted by the composer
As Albert Herring

Benjamin Britten *Billy Budd*, Op. 50
Libretto by E. M. Forster and Eric Crozier (after Herman Melville)
Royal Opera House, Covent Garden, 1 December 1951, conducted by the composer
As Captain Vere

Benjamin Britten *The Burning Fiery Furnace*, Op. 77
Libretto by William Plomer
Orford Church, 9 June 1966, with the English Opera Group (music under the direction
of the composer)
As Nebuchadnezzar

Benjamin Britten *Curlew River*, Op. 71
Libretto by William Plomer
Orford Church, 13 June 1964, with the English Opera Group (music under the direction
of the composer)
As The Madwoman

Benjamin Britten *Death in Venice*, Op. 88
Libretto by Myfanwy Piper (after Thomas Mann)
The Maltings, Snape, 16 June 1973, with the English Opera Group, artists of the Royal
Ballet and the Royal Ballet School and the English Chamber Orchestra, conducted by
Steuart Bedford
As Aschenbach

Benjamin Britten   *Gloriana*, Op. 53
Libretto by William Plomer
The Royal Opera House, Covent Garden, 8 June 1953, conducted by John Pritchard
As the Earl of Essex

Benjamin Britten   *A Midsummer Night's Dream*, Op. 64
Libretto, adapted from William Shakespeare, by Benjamin Britten and Peter Pears
Jubilee Hall, Aldeburgh, 11 June 1960, with the English Opera Group conducted by
the composer
As Flute

Benjamin Britten   *Owen Wingrave*, Op. 85
Libretto by Myfanwy Piper (after Henry James)
BBC Television, 16 May 1971, with the English Chamber Orchestra conducted by
the composer
As General Sir Philip Wingrave

Benjamin Britten   *Peter Grimes*, Op. 33
Libretto by Montagu Slater
Sadlers Wells Theatre, 7 June 1945, conducted by Reginald Goodall
As Peter Grimes

Benjamin Britten   *The Prodigal Son*, Op. 81
Libretto by William Plomer
Orford Church, 10 June 1968, with the English Opera Group (music under the direction
of the composer)
As The Tempter

Benjamin Britten   *The Rape of Lucretia*, Op. 37
Libretto by Ronald Duncan (after André Obey)
Glyndebourne, 12 July 1946, conducted by Ernest Ansermet
As Male Chorus

Benjamin Britten   *The Turn of the Screw*, Op. 54
Libretto by Myfanwy Piper (after Henry James)
Teatro la Fenice, Venice, 14 September 1954, with the English Opera Group, conducted
by the composer
As The Prologue and Quint

Dmitri Shostakovich   *The Lady Macbeth of Mtsensk*
Libretto by A. Preis and the composer, translated by M. D. Calvocoressi
Queen's Hall, London, 18 March 1936, with the BBC Chorus and Symphony Orchestra,
conducted by Albert Coates (concert performance)
As Second Foreman

William Walton   *Troilus and Cressida*
Libretto by Christopher Hassall
Royal Opera House, Covent Garden, 3 December 1954, conducted by
Sir Malcolm Sargent
As Pandarus

in twentieth-century realizations of eighteenth-century works

Benjamin Britten (realization)   *The Beggar's Opera*, Op. 43
a ballad opera by John Gay (1728)
Arts Theatre, Cambridge, 24 May 1948, with the English Opera Group, conducted by
Benjamin Britten
As Macheath

Arthur Oldham (realization)   *Love in a Village*
Ballad opera, with text by Isaac Bickerstaffe
Jubilee Hall, Aldeburgh, 16 June 1952, with the English Opera Group, conducted by
Norman Del Mar
As Hawthorn

Peter Pears in the Recording Studio: John Culshaw talks to Benjamin Britten at a play-back during the Decca recording sessions for *A Midsummer Night's Dream* at Walthamstow Town Hall, September 1966. Behind: John Mordler (left) and Gordon Parry (centre).

PETER PEARS:
THE RECORDED REPERTOIRE

Jeremy Cullum

In 1942, as an impressionable Cathedral choir boy, I was fortunate enough to hear one of the first 78 r.p.m. pressings of Peter Pears and Benjamin Britten performing the recently composed Michelangelo Sonnets. Little did I think that ten years later I would find myself working for them, and that one of my first tasks would be to make a card index of a large box of test pressings – including many *takes* of the Michelangelo Sonnets.

After more than seventeen years with them, and being involved in various minor ways with many recording sessions, I became the owner of a record shop which prides itself on having in stock all the available recordings by Peter Pears and Benjamin Britten. I think that their attitude to recordings was that of benevolent co-operation: they were both worried that one performance on a record could so easily become the only way of performing that work for its hearers, and this is born out by remarks I hear from browsing customers who are unwilling to have two recordings of the same Mozart piano concerto or Beethoven symphony. Thank goodness this feeling did not prevent them from putting on disc so many authoritative performances, with Ben conducting or playing the piano and – nearly always – Peter singing.

All who loved the song recitals these two great artists gave all over the world will agree that it is marvellous to be able to provide one's own recitals, although sadly there is at the moment no recording of them performing Purcell, an essential ingredient of any Britten–Pears recital.

But we are most grateful of all to Peter Pears for his recreation for the gramophone of all the marvellous and varied parts that were written for him in the Britten operas. Apart from the beauty and artistry of these outstanding performances, they give the final stamp of authority to these most important recordings.

We must not forget that, apart from his work with Benjamin Britten, there are also those unforgettable Evangelists in recordings of the Bach St Matthew and St John Passions, and also his performances in Stravinsky's *Oedipus Rex*, and Handel's *Acis and Galatea*, to name but a few. And we have had some superb records as a result of Peter Pears musical partnership with Julian Bream, performing songs from the Elizabethan lutenists, and more recently written songs with guitar.

What a rich and varied recording career Peter Pears has had, and what heartfelt thanks we must all offer him for it.

List Compiled by the Britten–Pears Library

This is designed to serve as a simple finding device rather than to stand as a systematic discography. Nevertheless, of course, it clearly displays the fascinating range and extent of Sir Peter's commercially-recorded repertory.

Accompanists, whether in the role of conductor, ensemble, instrumentalist or singer are indicated as briefly as possible. Opera casts are omitted. The dates given are dates of first publication rather than recording. All records are 33⅓ r.p.m. except where stated and where both stereophonic and monophonic recordings were made the stereo version only is indicated. Recordings which remain unissued are omitted. The list falls into three sections: I Peter Pears as singer. II Peter Pears as speaker. III Peter Pears as director of the Wilbye Consort. Record company codes in the following list may be elucidated by reference to the alphabetical index which appears quarterly in the Gramophone Classical Catalogue.

I   AS SINGER

ARNE	Ode in Honour of Great Britain – Rule Britannia I. Holst/Alde. Fest. (1953) LXT 2798

BACH	Cantata 67: Halt in Gedächtnis Jesum Christ
	    K. Richter/Munich (1960) SAWD 9904–B
	Cantata 108: Es ist euch gut, dass ich hingehe
	    K. Richter/Munich (1960) SAWD 9904–B
	Mass in B minor Jochum/Bav. RSO (1957)
	    Fontana 698002–3
	Matthäus-Passion Klemperer/Philh. (1962) SAXS 2446,
	    SAX 2447–50
	Matthäus-Passion Münchinger/Stuttg. (1965) SET 288–91
	St John Passion Willcocks/Philom. (1960) ZRG 5270–72
	St John Passion Britten/ECO (1972) SET 531–33
	Weihnachtsoratorium Münchinger/Stuttg.
	    (1967) SET 346–48

BEDFORD, D	Tentacles of the dark nebula D. Bedford/Lond. Sinf. (1974) HEAD 3
BENNETT	Tom o' Bedlam's Song Dickson (1964) ZRG 5418
BERKELEY, L	Four Ronsard Sonnets Op. 62a L. Berkeley/Lond. Sinf. (1974) HEAD 3 How love came in Britten (1956) LW 5241

BERLIOZ	L'Enfance du Christ Davis/Goldsborough SOL 60032–3

BRIDGE
Go not, happy day   Britten (1956) LW 5241
Goldenhair   Britten (1964) ZRG 5418
Journey's end   Britten (1964) ZRG 5418
Love went a-riding   Britten (1956) LW 5241
So perverse   Britten (1964) ZRG 5418
'Tis but a week   Britten (1964) ZRG 5418
When you are old   Britten (1964) ZRG 5418

BRITTEN
Albert Herring   Britten/ECO (1964) SET 274–6
Billy Budd   Britten/LSO (1968) SET 379–81
A Birthday Hansel   Ellis (1976) SXL 6788
The Burning Fiery Furnace   Britten/ECO (1967) SET 356
Cantata Academica   Malcolm/LSO (1962) SOL 60037
Cantata Misericordium   Britten/LSO (1965) SXL 6175
Canticle I   Britten (1962) ZRG 5277
Canticle II   Hahessy/Britten (1962) ZRG 5277
Canticle II   Baker/Johnson (1979) CBS 79316
Canticle III   Tuckwell/Britten (1962) ZRG 5277
Canticle III   Civil/Johnson (1979) CBS 79316
Canticle IV   Bowman/Shirley-Quirk/Britten
    (1973) SXL 6608
Canticle V   Ellis (1976) SXL 6788
Curlew River   Britten/ECO (1966) SET 301
Death in Venice   S. Bedford/ECO (1974) SET 581–3
Gloriana – The second lute song of the Earl of Essex
    Bream (1965) SB 6621
Gloriana – The second lute song of the Earl of Essex
    Ellis (1976) SXL 6788
The Holy Sonnets of John Donne   Britten (1949)
    HMV DB 6689–91 (78 rpm)
The Holy Sonnets of John Donne   Britten (1969) SXL 6391
Les Illuminations   Goossens/New SO (1954) LXT 2941
Les Illuminations   Britten/ECO (1967) SXL 6316
The Little Sweep   Britten/EOG (1956) LXT 5163
A Midsummer Night's Dream   Britten/LSO
    (1967) SET 338–40
Nocturne   Britten/LSO (1960) SXL 2189
On this Island – Let the florid Music praise   Britten (1956)
    LW 5241
On this Island   Britten (1982) REGL 417
Our Hunting Fathers   Britten/LSO (1982) REGL 417
Owen Wingrave   Britten/ECO (1971) SET 501–2
Peter Grimes   Britten/ROH (1959) SXL 2150–2
Peter Grimes – excerpts   Goodall/ROH (1972) RLS 707
The Prodigal Son   Britten/ECO (1970) SET 438
The Rape of Lucretia – excerpts   Goodall/Ch. Orch.
    (1948) HMV C 3699–706 (78 rpm)
The Rape of Lucretia   Britten/ECO (1971) SET 492–3
The Rape of Lucretia – excerpts   Britten/EOG (1981) IGI 369

Saint Nicolas   Britten/Alde. Fest. (1955) LXT 5060
Sechs Hölderlin-Fragmente   Britten (1963) SWL 8507
Serenade   Brain/Britten/Boyd Neel O (1945)
    AK 1151–3 (78 rpm)
Serenade   Brain/Goosens/New SO (1954) LXT 2941
Serenade   Tuckwell/Britten/LSO (1964) SXL 6110
Seven Sonnets of Michelangelo   Britten (1942) HMV B 9302
    and C 3312 (78 rpm)
Seven Sonnets of Michelangelo   Britten (1956) LXT 5095
Songs from the Chinese   Bream (1965) SB 6621
Spring Symphony   Britten/ROH (1961) SXL 2264
The Turn of the Screw   Britten/EOG (1955) LXT 5038–9
War Requiem   Britten/LSO (1963) SET 252–3
Who are these children?   Britten (1973) SXL 6608
Winter Words   Britten (1956) LXT 5095
Winter Words   Britten (1980) AF 001

BUSCH, W

Come, o come, my life's delight   Tunnard (1965) ZRG 5439
The Echoing Green   Tunnard (1965) ZRG 5439
If thou wilt ease thine heart   Tunnard (1965) ZRG 5439
The Shepherd   Tunnard (1965) ZRG 5439

BUSCH, A

Voices of the Prophets   A. Bush (1965) ZRG 5439

BUTTERWORTH

A Shropshire Lad – Is my team ploughing?   Britten (1956)
    LW 5241

BUXTEHUDE

O fröhliche Stunden   Malcolm (1961) SOL 60031
Nunc dimittis   Malcolm (1961) SOL 60031

CAMPIAN

Come let us sound with melody   Bream (1960) SXL 2191
Fair, if you expect admiring   Bream (1960) SXL 2191
Shall I come, sweet love?   Bream (1960) SXL 2191

COUPERIN

Audite omnes   Malcolm (1961) SOL 60031

DELIUS

To Daffodils   Tunnard (1965) ZRG 5439

DIBDIN
arr. Britten

Tom Bowling   Britten (1962) SEC 5102

DOWLAND

Awake, sweet love   Bream (1956) LW 5243
Fine knacks for ladies   Bream (1960) SXL 2191
I saw my lady weep   Bream (1956) LW 5243
If my complaints   Bream (1960) SXL 2191
In darkness let me dwell   Bream (1956) LW 5243
In darkness let me dwell   Bream (1966) SB 6646
The lowest trees have tops   Bream (1966) SB 6646
Say, love, if ever thou didst find   Bream (1966) SB 6646
Sorrow, stay   Bream (1960) SXL 2191
Sorrow, stay   Bream (1966) SB 6646
Time's eldest son   Bream (1966) SB 6646
What if I never speed   Bream (1960) SXL 2191
Wilt thou, unkind, thus reave me?   Bream (1966) SB 6646

ELGAR	The Dream of Gerontius Britten/LSO (1972) SET 525–6

FOLKSONG

arr Britten	The ash grove Britten (1944) 10009 (78 rpm – USA only)
arr Britten	The ash grove Britten (1955) LW 5122
arr Britten	The ash grove Britten (1962) SXL 6007
arr Britten	Avenging and bright Britten (1962) SXL 6007
arr Britten	La Belle est au jardin d'amour Britten (1962) SXL 6007
arr Copland	The Boatmen's dance Britten (1951) DA 7038 (78 rpm)
arr Grainger	Bold William Taylor Tunnard (1965) ZRG 5439
arr Britten	The Bonny Earl o' Moray Britten (1945) M 594 (78 rpm)
arr Britten	The Bonny Earl o' Moray Britten (1954) LW 5122
arr Britten	The Bonny Earl o' Moray Britten (1962) SXL 6007
arr Grainger	Brigg Fair S. Bedford/Linden Singers (1978) SXL 6872
arr Britten	A Brisk Young Widow Britten (1954) LW 5122
arr Britten	A Brisk Young Widow Britten (1963) SXL 6007
arr Britten	Ca' the Yowes Britten (1962) SXL 6007
arr Britten	Ca' the Yowes Ellis (1976) SXL 6788
arr Britten	Come you not from Newcastle? Britten (1947) HMV DA 1873 (78 rpm)
arr Britten	Come you not from Newcastle? Britten (1963) SXL 6007
arr Copland	The Dodger Britten (1951) DA 7039 (78 rpm)
arr Britten	Early one morning Britten (1962) SXL 6007
arr Britten	The foggy, foggy dew Britten (1947) HMV DA 1873 (78 rpm)
arr Britten	The foggy, foggy dew Britten (1962) SEC 5102
arr Britten	The foggy, foggy dew Britten (1980) AF 001
arr Britten	Heigh ho! Heigh hi! Britten (1945) M 594 (78 rpm)
arr Britten	How sweet the answer Britten (1962) SXL 6007
arr Copland	I bought me a cat Britten (1951) DA 7039 (78 rpm)
arr Britten	I married me a wife Ellis (1979) CBS 79316
arr Britten	I will give my love an apple Bream (1966) SB 6621
arr Britten	I will give my love an apple Bream (1979) CBS 79316
arr Seiber	J'ai descendu Bream (1966) SB 6621
arr Grainger	The jolly sailor song Bream (1950) DA 2032 (78 rpm)
arr Britten	The last rose of summer Britten (1962) SXL 6007
arr Britten	The Lincolnshire Poacher Britten (1962) SEC 5102
arr Britten	Little Sir William Britten (1944) M 555 (78 rpm)
arr Britten	Little Sir William Britten (1955) LW 5122
arr Copland	Long time ago Britten (1951) DA 7038 (78 rpm)
arr Grainger	Lord Maxwell's Goodnight Britten/ECO (1969) SXL 6410
arr Seiber	Marguerite, elle est malade Bream (1966) SB 6621
arr Britten	Master Kilby Bream (1966) SB 6621
arr Britten	Master Kilby Bream (1979) CBS 79316
arr Britten	The Miller of Dee Britten (1955) LW 5122
arr Britten	The Miller of Dee Britten (1962) SXL 6007
arr Britten	The Miller of Dee Britten (1980) AF 001
arr Britten	The Minstrel Boy Britten (1962) SXL 6007
arr Britten	O can ye sew cushions? Ellis (1976) SXL 6788
arr Britten	O waly, waly Britten (1950) HMV DA 2038 (78 rpm)
arr Britten	O waly, waly Britten (1962) SXL 6007

arr Britten	Oft in the stilly night	Britten (1962) SXL 6007
arr Britten	Oliver Cromwell	Britten (1944) M 555 (78 rpm)
arr Britten	Oliver Cromwell	Britten (1954) LW 5122
arr Grainger	The Power of Love	S. Bedford/ECO (1978) SXL 6872
arr Grainger	The Pretty Maid milkin' her Cow	Britten (1969) SXL 6410
arr Seiber	Réveillez-vous	Bream (1966) SB 6621
arr Britten	Le roi s'en va-t'en chasse	Britten (1950) RLS 748 (78 rpm)
arr Britten	Le roi s'en va-t'en chasse	Britten (1962) SXL 6007
arr Seiber	Le rossignol	Bream (1966) SB 6621
arr Britten	Sailor Boy	Bream (1966) SB 6621
arr Britten	The Salley Gardens	Britten (1944) M 555 (78 rpm)
arr Britten	The Salley Gardens	Britten (1955) LW 5122
arr Britten	Sally in our alley	Britten (1962) SEC 5102
arr Britten	She's like the swallow	Ellis (1979) CBS 79316
arr Britten	The shooting of his dear	Bream (1966) SB 6621
arr Copland	Simple gifts	Britten (1951) DA 7039 (78 rpm)
arr Grainger	Six dukes went a-fishin'	Britten (1953) HMV DA 2032 (78 rpm)
arr Grainger	Six dukes went a-fishin'	Ellis (1978) SXL 6872
arr Britten	The soldier and the sailor	Bream (1966) SB 6621
arr Grainger	The Sprig of Thyme	Britten (1969) SXL 6410
arr Britten	Sweet Polly Oliver	Britten (1946) M 678 (78 rpm)
arr Britten	Sweet Polly Oliver	Britten (1955) LW 5122
arr Britten	Sweet Polly Oliver	Britten (1963) SXL 6007
arr Britten	There's none to soothe	Britten (1946) M 678 (78 rpm)
arr Britten	There's none to soothe	Britten (1955) LW 5122
arr Grainger	The Three Ravens	S. Bedford/Linden Singers (1978) SXL 6672
arr Grainger	Willow, willow	Britten (1969) SXL 6410
FORD	Come, Phyllis, come	Bream (1960) SXL 2191
	Fair, sweet, cruel	Bream (1956) LW 5243
FRICKER	O Mistress Mine	Bream (1966) SB 6621
HANDEL	Acis and Galatea	Boult/Philom. (1960) SOL 60011–12
	L'Allegro ed il Penseroso	Willcocks/Philom. (1961) SOL 60025–6
	Ode for Saint Cecilia's Day – The trumpet's loud clangor; But bright Cecilia	Britten/ECO (1972) 5BB 119–20
— — —	Have you seen but a whyte lillie grow	Bream (1960) SXL 2191
HAYDN	Six Canzonets	Britten (1963) SWL 8507
HOLST, G	Four Songs	Brainin (1967) ZRG 5497
	Twelve Songs – Persephone	Britten (1956) LW 5241
	Twelve Songs	Britten (1968) ZRG 512
IRELAND	Friendship in misfortune	Britten (1964) ZRG 5418
	I have twelve oxen	Britten (1956) LW 5241

	The Land of lost content Britten (1964) ZRG 5418
	Love and friendship Britten (1964) ZRG 5418
	The One Hope Britten (1964) ZRG 5418
	The Trellis Britten (1964) ZRG 5418
LUTOSLAWSKI	Paroles tissées Lutosawski/Lond. Sinf. (1974) HEAD 3
——— arr. Oboussier	Miserere, my maker Bream (1960) SXL 2191
MOERAN	In youth is pleasure Britten (1956) LW 5241 The Merry Month of May Tunnard (1965) ZRG 5439
MORLEY	Come, sorrow, come Bream (1956) LW 5243 I saw my lady weeping Bream (1960) SXL 2191 It was a lover and his lass Bream (1956) LW 5243 Mistress mine, well may you fare Bream (1956) LW 5243 Thyrsis and Milla Bream (1960) SXL 2191 What if my mistress now Bream (1960) SXL 2191 With my love my life was nestled Bream (1960) SXL 2191
NORDHEIM	Doria Dreier/RPO (1979) HEAD 23
OLDHAM	Three Chinese Lyrics Britten (1956) LW 5241
PILKINGTON	Rest, sweet nymphs Bream (1960) SXL 2191
PUCCINI	Turandot Mehta/LPO (1973) SET 561–3
PURCELL ed. Britten & I. Holst	Dido and Aeneas S. Bedford/Alde. Fest. (1978) SET 615

ed. Lewis
ed. Britten & I. Holst
 	
real. Britten
	The Fairy Queen Lewis/Boyd Neel O. (1957) OL 50139–41
	The Fairy Queen Britten/ECO (1972) SET 499–500
	Morning Hymn Malcolm (1961) SOL 60031
	O Lord, grant the Queen a long life I. Holst (1953) LXT 2798
	The Queen's Epicedium Britten (1948) HMV DB 6763
	    (78 rpm)
	When the cock begins to crow Bowman/Shirley-
	    Quirk (1973) SXL 6608

RAINIER	Cycle for declamation (1964) ZRG 5418
ROSSETER	Sweet, come again Bream (1960) SXL 2191 What is a day? Bream (1960) SXL 2191 What then is love but mourning? Bream (1956) LW 5243 When Laura smiles Bream (1956) LW 5243 Whether men do laugh or weep Bream (1960) SXL 2191
SCHUBERT	Abendbilder Britten (1981) REGL 410 Abendstern Britten (1975) SXL 6722 Am See Britten (1944) 10009 (78 rpm – USA only) An die Entfernte Britten (1975) SXL 6722 An die Laute Britten (1961) SEC 5084 Atys Britten (1975) SXL 6722 Auf dem Wasser zu singen Britten (1975) SXL 6722

Auf der Bruck   Britten (1952) HMV DB 21423 (78 rpm)

Auflösung   Britten (1975) SXL 6722

Du bist die Ruh   Britten (1960) BR 3066

Der blinde Knabe   Britten (1981) REGL 410

Das war ich   Britten (1981) REGL 410

Der Einsame   Britten (1961) SEC 5084

Der Einsame   Britten (1975) SXL 6722

Geheimes   Britten (1961) SEC 5084

Der Geistertanz   Britten (1975) SXL 6722

Gesang des Harfners   Britten (1960) BR 3066

Die Götter Griechenlands   Britten (1981) REGL 410

Ihr Grab   Britten (1981) REGL 410

Im Frühling   Britten (1952) HMV DB 21423 (78 rpm)

Im Frühling   Britten (1975) SXL 6722

Lachen und Weinen   Britten (1975) SXL 6722

Licht und Liebe   Ameling/Baldwin (1979) CBS 79316

Das Lied im Grünen   Britten (1981) REGL 410

Der Musensohn   Britten (1960) BR 3066

Nacht und Träume   Britten (1975) SXL 6722

Nachtstück   Britten (1975) SXL 6722

Nur wer die Sehnsucht kennt   Ameling/Baldwin (1979)
    CBS 79316

Die schöne Müllerin   Britten (1960) SXL 2200

Schwanengesang – Die Stadt   Britten (1961) SEC 5084

Schwanengesang – Das Fischermädchen   Britten (1975)
    SXL 6722

Schwanengesang – Die Taubenpost   Britten (1961) SEC 5084

Sprache der Liebe   Britten (1975) SXL 6722

Der Winterabend   Britten (1981) REGL 410

Die Winterreise   Britten (1965) SET 270–1

SCHUMANN   Dichterliebe   Britten (1965) SET 270–1

Fünf Lieder Op. 40   Perahia (1979)   CBS 36668

Liederkreis Op. 39   Perahia (1979) CBS 36668

Scenes from Goethe's 'Faust'   Britten/ECO (1973)
    SET 567–8

Sechs Gedichte und Requiem Op. 90   Perahia (1979)
    CBS 36668

SCHÜTZ   Die Auferstehung unsres Herren Jesu Christi
    Norrington (1972) ZRG 639

Matthäus-Passion   Norrington (1972) ZRG 689

Paratum cor meum   Malcolm (1961) SOL 60031

Venite ad me   Malcolm (1961) SOL 60031

SHAKESPEARE   Twelfth Night (as Feste) (1961) ZRG 5284–6

SHIELD
arr Britten   The Plough Boy   Britten (1947) HMV DA 1873 (78 rpm)

arr Britten   The Plough Boy   Britten (1963) SXL 6007

arr Britten   The Plough Boy   Britten (1980) AF 001

STRAVINSKY	Oedipus Rex Stravinsky/Cologne RSO (1955) ABL 3054
	Oedipus Rex Solti/LPO (1978) SET 616
TIPPETT	Boyhood's End Mewton-Wood (1953) RG 15
	The Heart's Assurance Mewton-Wood (1953) RG 15
	Songs for Ariel Britten (1965) ZRG 5439
VAN DIEREN	Dream Pedlary Tunnard (1965) ZRG 5439
	Take, O take those lips away Tunnard (1965) ZRG 5439
VAUGHAN WILLIAMS	On Wenlock Edge Zorian Quartet/Britten (1948)
	M 585–7 (78 rpm)
WALTON	Anon in love Bream (1966) SB 6621
	Troilus and Cressida – How can I sleep? Walton
	(1968) SET 392–3
WARLOCK	Corpus Christi A. Wood/Woodgate (1936) K 827 (78 rpm)
	Along the stream Tunnard (1965) ZRG 5439
	Piggesnie Tunnard (1965) ZRG 5439
	Yarmouth Fair Britten (1956) LW 5241
— — —	Why was Lloyd George born so beautiful?
	P. Cranmer (1972) ISM
WEELKES	The Andalusian merchant (1969) SXL 6384
	As Vesta was . . . (1969) SXL 6384
	Ay me, alas, hey ho (1969) SXL 6384
	Cease now delight (1969) SXL 6384
	Cease sorrows now (1969) SXL 6384
	Hark all ye lovely saints (1969) SXL 6384
	Hark I hear some dancing (1969) SXL 6384
	Hence care, thou art too cruel (1969) SXL 6384
	Lady, the birds right fairly (1969) SXL 6384
	Like two proud armies (1969) SXL 6384
	My Phyllis bids me pack (1969) SXL 6384
	O care, thou wilt despatch me (1969) SXL 6384
	On the plains, fairy trains (1969) SXL 6384
	Say, dear, when will your frowning leave? (1969) SXL 6384
	Sing we at pleasure (1969) SXL 6384
	Strike it up, tabor (1969) SXL 6384
	Sweet love, I will no more abuse thee (1969) SXL 6384
	Ta ta ra, cries Mars (1969) SXL 6384
	Those sweet delightful lilies (1969) SXL 6384
	Though my carriage be but careless (1969) SXL 6384
	Thule, the period of cosmography (1969) SXL 6384
	Why are you ladies staying? (1969) SXL 6384
WILBYE	Adieu, sweet Amirillis (1974) SXL 6639
	All pleasure is of this condition (1971) 500275
	As fair as morn (1971) 500275
	Away, thou shalt not love me (1974) SXL 6639
	Come shepherd swains (1971) 500275
	Down in a valley (1971) 500275

Draw on, sweet night (1971) 500275
Flora gave me fairest flowers (1974) SXL 6639
Happy, o happy he (1971) 500275
Hard destinies are love and beauty parted (1971) 500275
Lady, when I behold (1974) SXL 6639
Lady, your words do spite me (1974) SXL 6639
Softly, o softly, drop mine eyes (1971) 500275
Stay, Corydon thou swain (1971) 500275
Sweet honey sucking bees (1971) 500275
There where I saw (1974) SXL 6639
Thus saith my Cloris bright (1974) SXL 6639
Unkind, o stay thy flying (1974) SXL 6639
Weep, weep mine eyes (1971) 500275
When shall my wretched life? (1974) SXL 6639
Ye that do live in pleasures plenty (1971) 500275
Yet sweet, take heed (1971) 500275

WOLF

An eine Aeolsharfe   Britten (1980) AF 001
Beherzigung   Britten (1981) REGL 410
Bei einer Trauung   Britten (1980) AF 001
Denk' es, o Seele!   Britten (1980) AF 001
Die du Gott gebarst   Britten (1981) REGL 410
Frühling übers Jahr   Britten (1981) REGL 410
Führ' mich, Kind   Britten (1981) REGL 410
Ganymed   Britten (1981) REGL 410
Der Gärtner   Britten (1981) REGL 410
Heimweh   Britten (1980) AF 001
Im Frühling   Britten (1980) AF 001
Jägerlied   Britten (1980) AF 001
Lied eines Verliebten   Britten (1980) AF 001
Sankt Nepomuks Vorabend   Britten (1981) REGL 410
Schlafendes Jesuskind   Britten (1981) REGL 410
Der Scholar   Britten (1981) REGL 410
Spottlied   Britten (1981) REGL 410
Wenn ich dein gedenke   Britten (1981) REGL 410
Wie sollt' ich heiter bleiben?   Britten (1981) REGL 410

II AS SPEAKER

BRITTEN

The Young Person's Guide to the Orchestra
    Markevitch/Philharm. (1955) CX 1175

KATHLEEN FERRIER

The Singer and the Person – Introduction (1979) REGL 368

SEIBER

Three Fragments from 'A Portrait of the Artist as a Young Man'
    Seiber/Melos (1960) SXL 2232

WALTON

Façade Sitwell/Collins/EOG (1954) LXT 2977

143

BRITTEN	Sacred and Profane (1977) SXL 6847
	A Shepherd's Carol (1977) SXL 6847
	Sweet was the song (1977) SXL 6847
	The Sycamore Tree (1977) SXL 6847
	A Wealden Trio (1977) SXL 6847
GIBBONS	Ah! Dear heart (1974) SXL 6639
	The silver swan (1974) SXL 6639
	What is our life? (1974) SXL 6639
TOMKINS	Adieu, ye city-prisoning towers (1974) SXL 6639
	Fusca, in thy starry eyes (1974) SXL 6639
	Music divine (1974) SXL 6639
	See, see the shepherds' queen (1974) SXL 6639
	Weep no more, thou sorry boy (1974) SXL 6639
	When David heard (1974) SXL 6639
	When I observe (1974) SXL 6639
	Yet again, as soon revived (1974) SXL 6639

Label from the 78 rpm HMV recording of Seven Sonnets of Michelangelo Op 22 made by Peter Pears and Benjamin Britten in September 1942.

THE BRITTEN–PEARS LIBRARY

The Britten–Pears Library consists of the working collection of books and music assembled by Benjamin Britten and Peter Pears. It also houses a large corpus of letters, photographs, printed programmes and a sound and video archive. Its principal distinction is the unique collection of Britten's manuscripts, including those belonging to the British Library which are deposited on permanent loan.

All enquiries relating to the Britten–Pears Library series of publications should be addressed to: Paul S. Wilson, Librarian, The Britten–Pears Library, The Red House, Aldeburgh, Suffolk IP15 5PZ.

Orders for Britten–Pears Library publications should be addressed to: Faber Music Limited, 3, Queen Square, London WC1N 3AU.